Dear Reader:

It is an honor to present *Harlem's Dragon* by David Rivera, Jr.; the first novel I acquired after Strebor Books International became an official imprint of ATRIA/Simon and Schuster. I came across the self-published version at a local Maryland bookstore, was blown away by the breathtaking cover, and had to read it. From cover to cover, I was a satisfied reader and I am sure you will be as well.

Rivera has a unique literary voice that will not only have you discussing this novel with many others but will have you anxiously awaiting the sequel, *The Street Sweeper*, which will be released during the fall of 2006. The main character, Chemah, who is of African-American and Latino descent, will have female readers falling in love with his compassion and his strength. Male readers will be able to relate to him as he balances love and romance with career and responsibility.

Margarita is a woman who some readers will love because she exhibits the uninhibited behavior many females yearn to unleash in themselves. Yet and still, others will dislike her or teeter back and forth between love and hate. That is what makes *Harlem's Dragon* such an intriguing must-read.

It is always a pleasure to discover new voices and I am excited about the career Mr. Rivera has in front of him. I would like to thank you for supporting one of the Strebor Books International titles and hope you will venture forth to enjoy many others. If you are interested in becoming an independent sales representative for Strebor Books International and earn a significant extra income while encouraging literacy among your family, friends, and coworkers, please send an email with "Opportunity" in the subject line to StreborBooks@aol.com.

Sit back in a cozy chair, adjust your reading light, and begin on the journey of Chemah and Margarita as they prove who is really the Dragon of Harlem.

Peace and Many Blessings,

Zane

Publisher
Strebor Books International
www.streborbooks.com

ZANE PRESENTS

David Rivera, Jr.

Harlem's Dragon

THE LOVE YOU CAN'T FIGHT

SBI

STREBOR BOOKS

NEW YORK LONDON TORONTO SYDNEY

Strebor Books
P.O. Box 6505
Largo, MD 20792
http://www.streborbooks.com

Harlem's Dragon © 2005 by David Rivera, Jr.

This book is a work of fiction. Names, characters, places and incidents are products of the author's imagination or are used fictitiously. Any resemblance to actual events or locales or persons, living or dead, is entirely coincidental.

ISBN-13 978-1-59309-056-2
ISBN-10   1-59309-056-0
LCCN 2005937060

Front cover design: Eion Saunders

Distributed by Simon & Schuster, Inc.
1230 Avenue of the Americas
New York, NY 10020
1-800-223-2336

First Strebor Books trade paperback edition February 2006

10 9 8 7 6 5 4 3 2 1

Manufactured and Printed in the United States of America

For information regarding special discounts for bulk purchases, please contact Simon & Schuster Special Sales at 1-800-456-6798 or business@simonandschuster.com

DEDICATION

This book is dedicated to my brother Raul "Starsky" Quinones
whom I love and admire for keeping me safe and unaffected
in the worlds we've lived in.

ACKNOWLEDGMENTS

Special thanks to Grandmaster Sam McGee and Master Dwayne McGee for inspiring me to write a story about a Hero who lives in Harlem USA.

To my dear friend Fatimah Gladden, for always telling me I have enough stories to write a book.

To my aunt Lydia Anglero who showed me a different world through books.

To my father, Jose "Chemah" Melendez, for making me the man that I am. Thanks to my mother, Nelida Nieves, for her guidance.

To my friends Dorothy Ellis and Tiwanda Brown, who read and helped edit my first manuscript, thank you for the encouragement.

A proud and resounding applause to my children—David, Chemah, and Tatsuya—whose combined personalities of intelligence, humor and sensitivity made up the characteristics of the hero of this story.

Peace and Love to my wife, Judith Lee-Sing Rivera, for taking care of the details.

To Kesana Branford for allowing her beauty to be captured for the sake of a book cover. Thanks to the creative eyes of John Gonzalez, and sincere appreciation to Eion Saunders for collaborating in the creation of the book cover.

To all the people who've passed through my life providing me with anecdotal material, THANK YOU.

"There is only one happiness in life; to love and be loved."

—GEORGE SAND

Prayer:

May the evil man be good.
May the good man find peace.
May he who finds peace be free.
And may he who is free make others free.

Chapter 1
It is what it is

Margarita Smith was in the throes of a very powerful orgasm. Unlike the average woman, she was not afraid to tell a man exactly how to make her come. The funny thing about it was that any time she told a man exactly what she wanted sexually, men always thought they had hit the jackpot. A smile would play on their faces as they tried to act indifferent, but she could always see the look that she recalls little boys have when they get what they wanted most on Christmas mornings.

Margarita loved to suck a dick. She always said it that bluntly, not for shock value but to let men know that her appetite for it was just as strong as theirs or more so. Her friends always used terms like "performing fellatio" or "going down on someone." Even some of her male friends found it hard to be as raw as her. They would use metaphors like "slobbin' the knob," "polishing the wood," or "buffing the helmet." She would say, "No, I just like to suck dick."

Margarita had received two degrees from Columbia University: a bachelor's in sociology and a master's of science in political science. All of her friends and associates were educated pseudo-intellectuals, and she fancied herself to be a proud, intelligent and self-reliant black woman. As such, she scrutinized her own behaviors as much or more than anyone else's. Realizing that her penchant for "sucking dick" was not exactly on par behavior, being a proud self-reliant black woman made her analyze herself even more.

In her self-analysis, Margarita realized that it wasn't so much an oral fixation that she had, as much as she loved the control that she exerted over men while she was performing oral sex on them. When she licked the tip of a dick slowly, she would always hear a moan of submission to her will. When she sucked just the head in her mouth with the vacuuming power of a Hoover, she would hear, "Ooh God," knowing she was their deity. When she lapped the whole underside of a man's dick with the flat of her tongue, she could see the man was concentrating intensely and solely on her. When she took a man's entire dick in her mouth and down her throat, she could see a man's shock and admiration at her feat. Whenever she stopped what she was doing, she would always hear some form of pleading or begging to continue. She stopped often because the begging is what made her vagina become soaked with its own passion.

She didn't particularly like the taste of cum, but swallowed it sometimes for the effect it had on her partners. The fact that she had caused a man to ejaculate and the energy that she sensed she was taking from him is what inevitably made her orgasm. It wasn't in the giving of pleasure that she gained her satisfaction but in the taking of control.

As Margarita's orgasm ebbed, she sat back against the baseboard of her bed looking down at her latest conquest. Raheem was not an unusual black man. In fact, he was very ordinary. She had met him at the Starbucks on 125th Street two months ago. While the clerk was making her chocolate mocha cappuccino, she had made eye contact with Raheem. He was playing chess with some older gentleman who kept busy talking to himself between each move he made.

As she walked out the door sipping on her decadent treat, Raheem had come stumbling after her introducing himself as Raheem Gaines, a medical supply salesman and chess aficionado. Raheem was six feet tall, with dull brown eyes and sported a low fade. He was good looking enough, but there was nothing spectacular about him.

He had invited her to the Sugar Shack for a drink that night. The Sugar Shack was a trendy nightspot for upwardly mobile blacks who were looking for a cultural haven in Harlem. They held poetry readings some nights; those were Margarita's favorite. She felt that men who were into poetry were more sensitive than other men, and she just loved her men extra sensitive. The night she and Raheem went was a jazz night. She enjoyed his company and a week later they became lovers.

Now as she looked at Raheem she realized that they had no future together. Raheem had absolutely no clue that he was about to be dumped. He reached out and caressed Margarita's smooth brown legs. Had he been sensitive at all he would have noticed that the shiver she exhibited when he did this was not one of delight, but of revulsion. Margarita always felt this way after a few months with only one lover. During the sexual act everything was cool, but immediately afterward she would see all of the man's faults.

In front of her now she didn't see an intelligent handsome black man. Instead Margarita saw a boring, scrawny, little-dick man with bunions and corns on both feet. She thought that if she had his dick in her mouth right now she would probably bite the head off. Instead she simply allowed him to continue his abrasive caresses. Margarita knew the quickest way of getting rid of a man. "Raheem, have you ever thought about having children?"

"Huh, what did you say?"

"I asked you if you've ever thought about having children," Margarita repeated. "Yeah, I've thought about it, I plan on having a couple someday."

"Why, you want to have my baby?" Raheem asked smiling like that cat that ate the canary.

"Well, it's not that I want to have your baby so much as I do want to have a baby, and being that I'm not on any birth control, and, those condoms we used aren't one hundred percent, I thought it might be worth talking about."

Raheem's smile faded so quickly, you might have thought someone had slapped him in the face. "Are you trying to tell me that you're pregnant?"

"No, I didn't say I'm pregnant," Margarita answered. "Nor am I planning to get pregnant, but if by some small miracle I do get pregnant, I will definitely keep it."

Raheem had been through this scene with other women before. Or so he thought. *Every time a black woman finds a man making a little money, and doing well for himself, she always tries to trap him off,* he thought. In his paranoia,

Raheem had forgotten a few small details. Foremost, Margarita made twice the money he made just in consulting fees, so why would she be concerned with the small change he made? Furthermore, with her connections she could only help his business. Without thinking he let the ignorance flow out of him like thick spit through a straw. Margarita had set the bait, and Raheem had swallowed the hook whole. "Listen, Margarita, I'm not ready to have no baby anytime soon so you better just forget about it."

Margarita had used this particular ruse to get rid of men before, and she had her next response ready. "What do you mean you're not ready? You didn't say that while you were fucking me. Anyway, I don't need you to have a baby. As a matter of fact, I don't need you at all."

It was only at that moment that Raheem realized what he was throwing away. "Wait a minute, baby, you don't mean that."

"Baby, I thought you didn't want any baby," Margarita snapped.

"That's not what I'm saying," Raheem tried to get a word in.

"I know exactly what you're saying," Margarita interrupted him again. "What do you think, I'm some kind of crack-head bitch you can give three dollars to and fuck her whenever you want?"

Raheem decided to use his business tone. It usually worked to make white people feel comfortable when he was doing business, and he used it whenever he needed to take control of a situation. "On the contrary, Margarita, I have nothing but the utmost respect for you. I don't think there's any reason to—"

"Just get the hell out," Margarita said.

Raheem got dressed quickly not wanting to incur Margarita's wrath anymore. He mumbled apologies the entire time he was dressing. It took all of the restraint that Margarita had to keep from laughing in his face. When he finally reached the door, Raheem said, "Margarita, I don't know what to say; please accept my apology." Raheem was begging now as much as he was begging fifteen minutes ago when she was sucking his dick.

That's the way Margarita liked her relationships with men from beginning to end. Her friends always joked with her about the intricate plotting that Margarita laid down whenever she was breaking it off with a man. "Why don't you just tell them you don't want them anymore?" they would continuously ask. Her friends never understood, but she always tried to explain how important it was to her that she control how and when her male friends went out of her life. After a while she would just answer, "You know my motto: always keep them begging for more." To Raheem, she said, "There's nothing more to say, Raheem. You've said more than I wanted to hear already." With that she closed the door in his face and locked both of the Medeco locks with a finality that comforted her.

Chapter 2
IN THE BEGINNING

The test was almost over. It had started an hour ago, and Chemah was exhausted. He could hear his own pulse, and feel his blood rushing through his body fueled by the adrenaline that his brain was releasing. He had been given a full two minutes to rest before the final and hardest part of the test is to begin. His *gi*, the formal Japanese name for a karate uniform, was sticking to his body. Soaked with sweat, it felt uncomfortable and cumbersome. Chemah turned his back to the small crowd that had come to witness his final promotion and knelt to compose himself. A few of his dreadlocks had come loose and hung in front of his face hiding the fire in his hazel-green eyes. He brushes them back with his right hand and is reminded that he cannot afford to be distracted when the test begins again. Loosening the ribbon that holds his dreads to the back of his head, he allows them to fall about his shoulders for half a second before tossing his head back and retying them into a ponytail.

This small movement did not go unappreciated by the women who were watching in the stands. "Damn, that brother is fine," a woman, wearing an African print dress with her hair cut into a short Afro, whispered to her friend. "Now you know you ain't never had no high-yella man before, with your ole back-to-Africa ass, so just stick to those Wesley Snipes-looking motherfuckers, and leave this brother to me." The woman with the Afro sucked her teeth and rolled her eyes but kept quiet, knowing she had just played herself.

Chemah closed his eyes to meditate and found that his mind would not be calmed so easily, as it drifted back to another time seventeen years earlier. He's ten years old and in the fifth grade. His class had been noisy during lunch so they were kept in longer than the rest of the students in Hans Christian Andersen School. Chemah's mind scattered even more as he wondered what kind of person this Hans Christian Andersen could have been that he could be white, and have a school named after him that was located on 122nd Street and Lenox Avenue. No one had ever told him that the school was named after a white man; he just figured with a name like Hans the guy had to be white.

By the time he was let out of school the whole sidewalk was congested with children. Some of the smaller kids had parents there to pick them up, but most didn't. The Mister Softee truck was in front of the school with music blasting but didn't get much business. Any kid with a quarter or more went to the little Spanish man who sold icees from a push cart and served them in Dixie cups. You could get coconut, cherry, mango, or rainbow flavors. Spanish people in the neighborhood called them *coquitos* because back in the day, they only came in coconut flavor. Nobody gave a shit about that. Now they're icees.

Chemah was walking with his icee extended in front of him, so not to mess up his school clothes, when he was pushed from behind and fell to the floor. He let go of the icee a split second before hitting the concrete so that he could use both hands to keep from losing his fronts. Without knowing or caring who pushed him down, he instinctively jumped to his feet and whirled around in a cat stance. Looking into the faces in front of him, he wished he had gone straight home like his father had told him. "Oh shit, it's on now," someone nearby said. Sonny Bermudez was the toughest kid in school, known to be a bully and didn't give a fuck if you were blind with one leg and your momma died. If he felt like kicking your ass, that was it. "Who you supposed to be, Bruce Lee motherfucker?" Raul spit from his mouth. Chemah stayed quiet squeezing his sphincter muscles to keep from shitting his pants. A crowd had already begun to form around them 'cause everyone likes to see an after-school fight. Simone, a little girl with braids, liked Chemah but couldn't help instigating. "Yo, Sonny, you better chill! That boy knows karate. I be seeing his father take him every week. He wears a black uniform and everything."

Sonny didn't seem to be fazed by this information. "What karate school do you go to, faggot?" he taunted Chemah.

"Harlem Goju," Chemah blurted.

"I ain't never heard of that shit," Sonny answered. The crowd laughed and squeezed in tighter making it impossible for Sonny to back out, or for Chemah to turn and run. "I know Puerto Rican Judo," Sonny said with a deadly smirk on his face. Chemah had never heard of that style and cautiously sunk deeper into his stance. "That's right, Judono if I have a knife; Judono if I have a gun; Judono anything."

The crowd laughed and as if on cue Sonny lunged at Chemah with his head down. Chemah snapped out his lead leg with a front kick that caught Sonny in the forehead. Sonny staggered backward and looked as if he were about to cry. Having gained some confidence after that first kick, Chemah settled back in his cat stance and waited for Sonny to attack again. This time Sonny launched a wild round-house punch that Chemah stopped with a shuto block.

That's the last thing Chemah remembered of the fight. As it was told to him later, one of Sonny's boys had snuck up on him and put him in the dope fiend yoke. "You know it only takes four seconds in that kind of head lock to put a nigga's head to bed. Then they just gave you a 125th Street beatdown," they had informed him when he was let out of the hospital.

The memory was a reminder that he could never let his guard down during this test. He breathed deeply and evenly as he gathered his energy and rested his body and mind.

He knew his two minutes would be up when Grandmaster Sam McGee rapped his bamboo staff on the floor twice. Silence was instant and tension was felt by everyone in the gym as they waited to see the last part of the test. Half of the crowd was martial artists who wanted to witness the making of a fifth-degree black belt. The other half were just Harlem residents who were brought to what they believed was a karate show. To them it may just as well been the Apollo

Theater. If they liked what they saw, they'd clap and if they didn't like what they saw, fuck it, they were gonna let you know.

Chemah knew what to expect: the fight of his life. In the Chinese movies you see all kinds of shit passing as a test to become a master. A guy catching arrows with his teeth. Snatching a coin from your master's hand. In Harlem Goju, they're keeping it real. You wanna be a fifth-degree. They're not giving shit away. You have to fight someone who's already a master. If you don't hold your own and can't at least come close to beating your opponent, you're going to have to try again in a couple of years. That determination can only be made by the Grandmaster. You think it's gonna be a long fight, it's not. Any master will tell you if a fight is not over in four moves or less neither man knows what he is doing. It's like a high-speed chess game only at this high level the man you're playing against can remove your testicle, gouge out an eye, dislocate your shoulder, or give you a 125th Street beatdown.

Chemah stepped into the fighting circle keenly aware that the man in front of him was capable of taking his life. His presence was huge. He was unknown to most in the audience, but Chemah knew he was Master John Charlotte of the Tiger Claw karate school in California. The elders of the Harlem Goju system agreed that Chemah should not fight someone from their ranks so that it would be a real test with no holding back. It took some time to find anyone willing to fight Chemah as he had won most of his tournament fights since he had become a black belt at ten years old. Some people now referred to him as the Dragon of Harlem. But this was different. This was for honor and respect. Only someone with honor and respect would agree to be your opponent.

Both opponents simultaneously bowed to grandmaster Sam McGee and then bowed to one another without ever taking their eyes off of each other. There were no other formalities to observe and both men were immediately on the offensive.

Chemah launched an attack of four consecutive straight punches. Master Charlotte avoided them with what seemed like nonchalance, his head moving from side to side. Chemah's fist missed him each time by just a fraction of an inch. Master Charlotte stepped inside of Chemah's right foot and Chemah saw the master's palm strike headed straight for his chest. Chemah's right hand shot out to disrupt the palm strike, realizing a split second too late that the palm was merely a decoy for the real attack. Master Charlotte had set him up for a dragon sweep, which he fell for hook, line and sinker. Chemah found himself airborne and out of control, knowing he would land on his head if he did not torque his full body weight. He maneuvered at the last instant and landed on his side. The pain of the landing hit him with the force of a sledgehammer, but he jumped up and continued to fight as if nothing had happened.

Pain control was one of the many disciplines of Goju, but he had learned to control pain many years ago, when his mother was whipping his ass with one of the tracks of his racing-car set. His mother prefaced every beating he had earned with, "And you better not cry." If you can take a Hot Wheels track hitting you in between every two words your mother is screaming…*"I told you…SMACK! …not to…SMACK!…go out…SMACK!…side…SMACK!…without… SMACK! …my…SMACK!… permission."*

"I'm sorry, Mommy, I'm sorry. I won't do it again."

"I know…SMACK! …you won't…SMACK!…do it again…SMACK!…'cause you shouldn't…SMACK!…have done it to begin…SMACK!…with."… then it's a good bet that you can probably take a couple of shots from a black belt without too much trouble. Chemah attempted a spinning back kick to Master Charlotte's head only to find himself again soaring through the air out of control. Chemah was running out of time; another hit like the last one and he knew it would be over.

Grandmaster Sam McGee had always said, "I can teach you karate, but you must make it your own." Until this moment, he hadn't fully realized what that meant. Don't fake like you some punk-ass Japanese soldier. You're from Harlem; do what you do best.

There is a little known style of fighting that some say originated in Harlem and others say originated on Rikers Island—the biggest jail in the world. It was hard to master, but Chemah was taught by his Uncle Raul "Starsky" Quinones. His uncle had been a well-respected but hardened man who had a reputation for causing pain. This style was called the 52 steps. Chemah had always toyed with combining both styles to make a new fighting system but thought it would offend the Grandmaster.

"Fuck it. I'm getting my ass waxed; this shit stops now." Chemah circled his opponent slowly and started the intricate pattern of hand movements that make up the 52 steps. Master Charlotte was looking at Chemah like he was crazy, and got ready to finish what he started. Chemah's uncle taught him to always talk shit to his opponent while fighting. "It scares the shit outta motherfuckas and it gives you a rhythm to move with," he'd said. Chemah knew that he could not talk out loud, but his eyes and attitude spoke with volume. "You don't know who you fucking with *(elbow strike to the head)*. You don't know me *(slap to the face)*. What's my name *(back fist)*? What's my name *(back fist)*?"

Charlotte was seeing three hands, coming at him with crazy speed. He believed he had found the rhythm Chemah's hands were moving in when he was hit by a Goju thunder kick to his temple. The fight was over. Master Charlotte was helped to his feet and out of the dojo. The ceremony continued.

The audience went crazy stomping the floor, clapping their hands, and whistling. "Yo, did you see that shit? He went straight uptown on his ass."

"Yeah, I saw. I knew he was gonna do his thing. That brotha's from 'round the way."

Grandmaster Sam McGee tapped his bamboo staff on the floor twice and once again commanded the attention of everyone in the gym with his presence. "I would like to thank everyone who has come to share with us this great occasion, in which…" Sam McGee began.

The rest of the words were lost to Chemah whose attention was drawn to a single face in the crowd. It was Khadijah Saeed. She had come to see him earlier that week about helping in her campaign for city council. She was running against Charles Rangel's crew and she had asked him to help her get the votes from the City College student population. Chemah had graduated from there, but was still very popular with the students, as he still used many of their lab facilities for projects he had little funding for. Khadijah always rolled with a small group of beautiful black women. Today was no different; every woman sitting around her was a dime piece. Khadijah was usually the finest of them all. Today was no different except the sister sitting to her immediate right could damn sure give her a run for her money. Chemah admired her smooth chocolate skin and long hair. He immediately wondered if it was all hers.

"It is my honor to bestow upon you the rank of fifth-degree black belt." The Grandmaster's voice brought him back to the event at hand.

Chemah was handed his new belt which held the colors black, white, and red. Chemah bowed accepting the new belt; he took off his old black belt and reverently handed it to the Grandmaster. "Thank you, Grandmaster." Chemah humbly bowed.

Grandmaster Sam McGee leaned close to Chemah and whispered, "You can thank me by telling me what those last few moves were."

"Uh, you mean those last moves at the end of the fight?" Chemah said, stuttering and stalling. "Didn't you recognize them, Grandmaster?" Chemah smiled.

Grandmaster Sam McGee folded his arms and slowly shook his head patiently waiting for an explanation. Chemah flashed his most charming smile and tried to sound casual. "The moves were from a new kata I came up with. I thought I'd wait until after I became a master to show it to you, but I guess it couldn't wait. I call it 'The 52 steps of Harlem Goju.'"

Chapter 3
THAT'S JUST MY LUCK!

Sensei Dwayne McGee was the brother of the Grandmaster and second in charge at Harlem Goju. He was five feet nine and arguably heavier than a martial arts master should be. The few people who made the mistake of thinking that his girth would hinder him from whipping their ass would remember him for the rest of their lives. Sensei Dwayne approached Chemah during Thursday night class and asked to see him after class was dismissed.

When the class was over, Chemah walked over to Sensei Dwayne, who was getting dressed in a corner of the dojo. "You wanted to see me, Sensei?" Chemah asked.

"I need you to go to Felix Robin's school tomorrow and find out from his teacher why he's failing so many classes."

The Sensei got right to the point. It was Sensei Dwayne McGee's habit to visit the school and teacher of any child who was not doing well in school. His ability to scare children into doing their best was rivaled only by his uncanny ability to find what motivated an individual and help them use that motivation.

As far as Chemah knew he had never asked anyone else to make one of these visits, and Chemah wasn't feeling especially honored that he asked him to be the first. "Sensei, I'm not sure that I can do it, I have a lot of things—"

"When you accepted Grandmaster's promotion of you to the fifth degree, you accepted all responsibilities that come with it, did you not?"

"Yes, Sensei."

"Are you now ready to turn your back on your fellow brothers? How many times have you heard Grandmaster say, 'When we make it to the top of the mountain, sometimes we have to turn around and help the man behind us reach the top.' Do you remember that?"

"Yes, Sensei, but—"

"This is not a task I like to give anyone. It's one of my many duties as Sensei that I thoroughly enjoy. The only reason I'm asking you to go in my place is that I've been called on an emergency out of town, and I've already told his teacher that I would be there. It's our job to help parent these children that are under our care, even outside of the karate school. All I need you to do is introduce yourself to the teacher as a representative of Harlem Goju. Make my apologies for not being able to make it and tell her that I will be in to visit as soon as I can. Now do you think you can handle that?" This man had been pushing Chemah's buttons for twenty years now, and knew that nothing would motivate him more than questioning his sense of responsibility.

"Yes, Sensei. What school is it and what is the teacher's name?" Chemah asked.

"It's your old school, Hans Christian Andersen, and the teacher's name is Nairobi Kimble," Sensei Dwayne said, turning his back to Chemah. After a moment of silence, Sensei Dwayne looked over his shoulder and saw Chemah still standing there. "Is there something else I can do for you?" he asked. Chemah shook his head no and his Sensei went back to dressing. Chemah knew that this meant he was dismissed.

Chemah walked into the school thirty minutes late and was surprised at how easy it was for an unidentified man to gain access into a building full of children. It was the end of the school day, and the halls were empty but for a few straggling boys going from room to room peeping into each door. Chemah took his cue from them, and went from door to door peering into each one looking for an adult to question about Miss Kimble's whereabouts. In the third room that he peeped in, there was a young white woman sitting at the teacher's desk appearing to be marking papers. Chemah knocked on the door before stepping over the threshold. "Pardon me," he said.

She looked up from her work. "Yes, how can I help you?" She had a natural and alluring smile.

"I'm looking for Miss Kimble. You wouldn't happen to know where she is, would you?"

"I'm Miss Kimble," she answered getting up from her desk and simultaneously whisking a strand of hair from her face.

"I'm sorry, I'm looking for Ms. Nairobi Kimble."

Her smile became broader as she came from behind her desk extending a hand. "That would still be me." She laughed. "And you must be Mr. McGee." She had caught Chemah off guard. He had fully expected Ms. Nairobi Kimble to be a Black woman.

"Yes, I mean, no. My name is Chemah Rivers. I'm one of Mr. McGee's students. Mr. McGee was called away on urgent business, and he asked that I make his apologies, and ascertain how we could best help Felix Robins." Chemah knew how important it was that Felix see that someone cared enough to come to school on his behalf, but it was too late for that part of the assignment. There would be no excusing it to Sensei when Chemah saw him again.

"Well, Mr. Rivers, I was hoping that Mr. McGee was coming to the school to have a talk with Felix. You see, last year, another teacher had a similar problem with a child, and Mr. McGee showed up out of nowhere and introduced himself as the child's Sensei, and asked to speak to her concerning the child's grades. He spoke to the child briefly before he left, but for the rest of the year the child was an exemplary student. I don't know what he said to the child but I was hoping for another one of Mr. McGee's miracles." Miss Kimble seemed genuinely concerned. Chemah could see the hurt in her eyes when she talked about not being able to reach the child, and the anger and frustration when she talked about parental involvement being non-existent.

"Maybe I can come back tomorrow at an earlier time, and have a little talk with Felix."

"That would be fine, Mr. Rivers. I'd appreciate that very much."

"It's no problem. You know I went to this school when I was little," Chemah said in an attempt to make small talk.

"It's hard to imagine you ever being little, Mr. Rivers."

Chemah could feel his ears burning and knew they were turning red! *Maybe it's time to leave,* he thought. But he didn't go anywhere.

He was enjoying the way Miss Kimble was looking at him. It was as if she were appreciating every muscle of his body and every wrinkle in his clothing. "You must work out a lot," she said. She had been watching the muscles play underneath his clothing with every movement that he made from the moment he knocked on the door.

"It's the karate. It keeps me in pretty good shape. Do you work out?" Chemah asked. Taking the opportunity to look at her from head to toe, he took inventory of all her assets. Five feet seven inches, about one hundred-fifty pounds, nice-sized breasts, and wide hips. Chemah found himself wishing she would turn around so that he could see her ass. *Nothing worse than a flat-ass woman.*

Miss Kimble let out a girlish giggle that even she did not recognize as her own, as his eyes swept over her body. "No, I don't have time to work out," she said. "But I've been thinking about joining a gym before my body gets out of control."

"It doesn't look that bad to me," Chemah said, holding her eyes with his own. Chemah had never flirted with a white woman before, but now it seemed as if color didn't matter. This woman was looking at him the way other women had, and he was talking and flirting with her the same way he would with any sister who was giving him good vibes. It was all good.

Miss Kimble broke their eye lock, and began gathering her belongings. "I'm pretty much finished here. So I guess I'll see you tomorrow and you'll have that talk with Felix." She slipped her shoulder bag over her arm and picked up a small box that was next to her desk. She subtly gestured that he walk toward the door ahead of her.

"Let me carry that box to your car for you," Chemah offered.

"I don't have a car. I take the bus."

"The *bus?*" Chemah repeated as if she had just said the most incredulous thing he had ever heard.

"Is there something wrong with taking the bus, Mr. Rivers?" she said, holding one eyebrow higher than the other in imitation of The Rock.

"*No,* there's nothing wrong with taking the bus. But, if you don't mind my asking, where do you live? I don't imagine that you live anywhere close to here."

"Eighty-Fourth Street Central Park West," she said as he liberated the box from her arms.

"Oh," he said, taken aback by her answer.

"Is there something wrong with where I live, Mr. Rivers?"

"No," he lied. "It's just that when you said you take the bus, I envisioned that you lived close by."

"Eighty-Fourth Street is not that far away."

"I'm sorry; I'm getting too personal," Chemah apologized.

"Not at all, Mr. Rivers. You do have to know where I live if you're going to drive me home. That is what you had in mind, isn't it?"

"As a matter of fact, I hadn't even considered it," Chemah continued to lie. As soon as those words came out of his mouth, he knew that it was the wrong thing to say. The smile that was on her face from the minute they had seen each other was gone. In its place was an expression of hurt and embarrassment. For reasons that he hadn't fathomed, he wanted to be the one to take that pained expression off of her face.

"I guess it's my turn to apologize," she said. "I assumed too much, I'm sorry."

"It's not that I don't want to take you home. It's just that I hadn't thought that anyone as beautiful as you would allow me to get that close." This was not a lie. There really was something beautiful about her. She wasn't gorgeous in the way that fashion models are, but exuded a sexiness that he believed came from being natural in her expression of emotion. It seemed she did everything and said everything with passion. Chemah noticed that as he spoke these eloquent words, the smile he was hoping for instantly came back to her face.

"That all depends on what you mean by close," she said, still smiling. "What I mean is—"

"Let's talk about it in the car," she interrupted as she walked out of the class in front of him. As he followed her he got a chance to thoroughly scrutinize her ass. Suffice to say it did not have the roundness to it that he enjoyed seeing a well-endowed sister showing off. But on the other hand, it did have some substance. Her Liz Claiborne skirt was clinging to it so that every step she took was akin to following a bouncing ball.

"Lose something," she said, looking over her shoulder. She had caught him staring at her buttocks and she continued to smile. Chemah was baffled. The few times he had chanced a look at a white woman's body, and she noticed, all he had gotten were some dirty looks. Here was a white woman he had not met more than an half-hour earlier, and he could tell she was feeling him, as much as he was feeling her.

As they exited the school, he pointed to his ride. "That's my car, there."

"BMW 650, very nice," she said, slowing her step to admire the car in its entirety.

Chemah was extremely proud of this car, but to her, he said, "It's okay." He paused. "There's just one thing I must insist on before you get into this car."

"And what would that be, Mr. Rivers?"

"That's exactly it. You've got to stop calling me Mr. Rivers. My name is Chemah."

"Alright, Shemur."

Chemah laughed because everyone initially said his name wrong. "No, not Shemur," he mimicked. "Chem with *ch* sound; *ahh* as if you were sighing," he pronounced.

"Chemah, Chemah," she repeated after him, this time saying the name perfectly. "Chemah, my name is Nairobi."

"Pleased to meet you, Nairobi. Nairobi, would you please do me the honor of allowing me to drive you home along the park?"

"Why, Chemah, I would be delighted."

They both got into the car laughing hysterically. They were still laughing as Chemah pulled from the curb and headed for Central Park.

Chapter 4
You know my style

Margarita was on the phone long distance with her father for the third time that day. A year earlier, he had retired back to Panama where Margarita herself was born. Margarita's father was worried about his daughter. He knew she had taken on all of the family's matriarchal needs since her mother had died; assuming a leadership role among her two sisters and brother had not been easy. *"Si, Papi,* no I'm okay, *no te apure.* Don't worry," she said in her broken Spanish and then hung up the phone.

She always felt emotionally drained after talking to her father. He insisted on speaking to her in Spanish hoping to remind her of her Panamanian heritage, but Margarita had always rebelled against it. Margarita had gained a sense of her blackness when she had first come to the States and was called "Blackey" by white girls in her neighborhood. They had loved to play with her long straight black hair, but she was never allowed in their homes. As more black girls mobbed into her neighborhood, she naturally gravitated toward being one of them. She would all but deny being Panamanian when friends came over to her house and said, "Your mother talks funny, where's she from?" Margarita eventually joined a Black political group in college; looking back she realized she had acceptance issues and low self-esteem because of those little white girls so long ago.

Just as Margarita hung up the phone, her friend and co-worker Kat burst through her office door. "Guess what?" she asked.

"What?" Margarita said.

"Guess," she repeated.

"I don't feel like playing this game now, Kat; just tell me what the hell is up." Kat was the computer specialist in the office; she was very bright and extremely ghetto. Being the only other Black woman in the small firm, she and Margarita were thick as thieves. "Your man is going to be at Thursday's fund-raiser," Kat squealed.

"And what man would you be referring to, Miss Kat?"

"What man?" Kat almost shouted. "The man. Fine Ass, dreadlock, high-yellow Hong Kong Phooey. That's what man." Kat had the annoying habit of going straight "ghetto" whenever she got too excited. Many times Margarita had to remind her that they were at their place of work, and not the PJs.

Margarita immediately perked up when she heard Kat's new gossip. "How did you find out?"

"I was talking to Sheila at Khadijah Saeed's office and she was talking about this fine man that might be helping Khadijah with her campaign. Anyway, when she described him I realized it was the same man. And for a nominal fee, I'll even tell you his name."

"And what makes you think I'm at all interested in his name?"

"Well, alright if you're not interested. I'll just take myself right back to my computer, and forget all about him," Kat said as she turned toward the door.

"Alright, alright," Margarita conceded. "What's your price?"

"Your blue dress."

"My blue Donna Karan dress?" Margarita asked. "You must be buggin'." Margarita could go "ghetto," too. "I ain't wore the thing but once."

"I just want to borrow it. I have a date with Stewart this weekend and I don't have anything special to wear," Kat begged.

Margarita thought for a moment. "Alright, you can wear it, but just one, and I want it back dry-cleaned. You damage it, you bought it. Deal?"

"Deal," Kat said, smiling.

"Don't just stand there, what's his name?" Margarita demanded.

"Chemah," Kat blurted.

"Shem who?" Margarita said, looking puzzled.

"Not Shem who, Chemah."

"Chemah," Margarita repeated, letting the name roll off her tongue. She smiled to herself. It was actually a beautiful name for a very beautiful man.

"Well, when do I get the dress?" Kat broke into her silence.

"I'll bring it with me tonight. You can get it from my trunk after the fundraiser is over."

At exactly five p.m., Margarita got up from her desk and started to make her way home. Initially, she was going to take a cab home from her office on Fifty-Ninth Street and Fifth Avenue. She thought of the rush-hour traffic and decided to take the train home instead. She walked the three blocks to Columbus Circle and waited on line to buy a token. Margarita was feeling especially giddy and she knew it was due to the prospect of getting close to this Chemah person. As Margarita stood on the platform, she visualized the first thing she would say when she was introduced to Chemah.

She smiled to herself. Anyone looking at her would have thought her demented or extremely happy. When the "D" train arrived, Margarita got on as if in a trance. When she reached her stop at 145th Street she took the steps out of the subway at a brutal pace considering the high-heeled shoes she was wearing. Margarita got out of the subway station and marched up Sugar Hill to Convent Avenue. Making a left on Convent, she walked one more block to her home.

Margarita had lived in Midtown two years before, and had found she was uncomfortable in her surroundings most of the time. While visiting a friend who lived uptown in the Strivers Row section of Harlem, she had been introduced to this particular part of Harlem where she now lived. She had bought her brownstone from a couple who were getting divorced and could not decide who was getting the house. The place was not in particularly bad condition, but needed some work. It was four stories and had been renovated as a four-unit dwelling. Upon buying the home, Margarita had rid herself of each of her tenants. She hired a broker to find them new apartments, and paid for their first two months' rent. When the last of the tenants left, the contractors came in immediately. She wanted the four-story, four-unit home restored to its original function as a single-family home. It had taken a full year to complete. She had lived in and around the construction the whole year. Some people thought she did it to save money on another apartment, but the truth is she wanted to oversee the entire project. Although she knew little to nothing about construction when the project started, she knew her home, top to bottom, inside and out when it was over.

Initially, the contractors had been annoyed with Margarita's constant questioning, but she won them over with her consistency and the speed in which she learned. She had done some research at Home Depot to ensure that all the materials used to reconstruct her home were of the highest quality. When it was completed she felt secure in the knowledge that she had helped build this home, and one day would raise a family here.

Margarita opened the door to her brownstone and as always the place seemed to welcome her. She took a deep breath and exhaled slowly, allowing the comfort of her home to take away the stresses of her office. Her routine was always the same. She walked into her living room and placed her keys and briefcase on the fireplace. She plopped down on her cherry-red living room couch and turned on her answering machine via the cordless phone she always left in the same corner of the couch. She was surprised to find that no one had called her, but was also relieved. She wanted to prepare herself for tonight's fund-raising dinner and did not want to be interrupted.

Margarita climbed the flight of stairs that led to the room she used as an office; the connecting room was a gym. Margarita knew that when she got married and had a family these rooms would become bedrooms for her children. She had planned it this way. It would give whoever she married a way of making the house part of them. She and he would design and decorate the children's bedrooms together, and then decorate the entire walk-in apartment space which she had left as a loft space, open and unencumbered by unnecessary walls. This would be a space whose use would be designated by her husband. *Hopefully, it will be an office. In the meantime, I'll use the second floor,* she had thought.

Margarita sat in front of the computer in the room she used as her home office and registered on the Internet. After a few minutes of searching, she found what she wanted. It was a site which, when given a name, would research the background of the name and tell you its meaning. It would also give you personality characteristics that the person with the name should possess. She typed the name onto the screen and in seconds her screen was full. It read: Chemah: Meaning— the Pacifier; Characteristics: focused, attentive, kind, passionate etc… Margarita knew this website was a hustle like many others. The characteristics that they produced were applicable to almost anyone. The meaning of the name, on the other hand, was something that she could use. It was a conversation piece. She thought out loud, "Chemah, the Pacifier. Well, I haven't had a pacifier in my mouth since I was two years old," she joked with herself.

Margarita got up from her computer and walked up one flight to her bedroom. Her walk-in closet was full of clothes that might do for a fund-raising event, but her choice of garments for this evening had to elicit a response from the one man she was interested in—Chemah. As she rummaged in her closet, she recited her new mantra. She started to chant, "Chemah, Chemah, Chemah…"

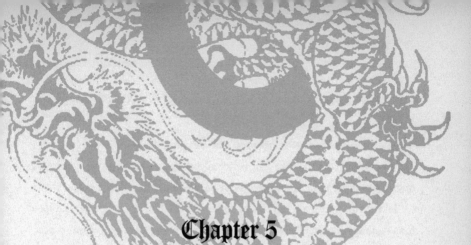

Chapter 5
WHO STOLE THE COOKIE FROM THE COOKIE JAR?

"Two-Ninety Central Park West," Chemah announced. "Last stop." He and Nairobi were still making silly jokes with each other.

"Would you like to come upstairs?" Nairobi asked, her face turning serious again. Chemah wanted to say yes, but tried to play it cool again. "I'll never find a parking space out here, I'd better just go," he said.

"Is it because I'm white?" she asked plainly.

"Because you're white?" Chemah repeated.

"Yeah, because I'm white, you think we shouldn't be together," Nairobi said genuinely.

"I never even thought about the color situation, Nairobi," Chemah said honestly. "I just move cautiously whenever I deal with women. We just met an hour ago and I thought maybe we were moving too fast."

"Too fast for what?" she snapped.

"Too fast to get to know each other better. Too fast for two people that obviously have chemistry to have a glass of wine?"

"Listen, Chemah, I keep my life very simple. If I don't like you, I stay away from you. If I like you, then I want you around me. Life is too short, and I plan to enjoy every minute that I can. I know you like me, so stop fronting."

Chemah laughed at her attempt to use slang.

"Yes, stop fronting," she repeated.

"Nairobi, are you trying to say frontin'?"

"That's what I said," she repeated, "fronting."

Chemah laughed again. "Your ebonics are terrible," he said. "Who's been teaching you this awful slang?"

"My students teach me sometimes," she said proudly.

"Then by all means…We had better spend more time together, you really ought to practice more. Your pronunciation is deplorable." They both laughed.

"I'll tell you what," she said. "You go around the block a few times, and look for a parking spot; that'll give me some time to tidy the place up. I wasn't expecting any company, and I left the place a mess this morning."

"OK," Chemah said this time. "I'll bring your box upstairs."

"I'll let the doorman know I'm expecting you. Don't take too long."

"What apartment?" Chemah screamed after her.

"Fifteen A," she called over her shoulder.

Twenty minutes later Chemah was in the elevator on his way up to Nairobi's apartment. The doorman had been expecting him and attempted to take the box from his arms. "Thank you. I'll take it up myself," he assured him.

"Yes, sir," the doorman said, being accommodating.

Chemah looked up and down the hall as he stepped off the elevator and stood in the middle of the hall. He saw the apartment number 15A approximately ten feet away to his left. He walked to the door, but as he reached to touch the doorbell, the door swung inward.

Nairobi stood at the threshold to the door and smiled. "Come in, the coast is clear." She had changed her clothes. She wore gray sweat pants and a T-shirt. Chemah looked at her from head to toe and saw that she was barefoot. Her feet were well pedicured. Chemah and his friends always discussed how important it was for a woman to have nice feet. Chemah crossed the doorway and walked down a hallway littered with pictures on the wall. Chemah noticed that Nairobi was in most of the pictures; the other people he guessed were family members. The living room was immense. It housed two huge bookcases opposite each other; they ran wall to wall, and floor to ceiling. Neither one looked as if it could house another book.

"Make yourself comfortable," Nairobi said. "I'll get us some wine."

Chemah sat on a couch that he thought he had seen in an IKEA catalog, and Nairobi came into the living room with two glasses of wine. "You haven't read all of these books, have you?" he asked.

"No, I inherited them from my family," she said as she handed Chemah a glass and sat close to him. "Ninety-five percent of them were already here when I got here."

"So this is your family's apartment?" he asked.

"No, it's my apartment. It used to belong to my grandmother, and she put me on the lease. When she died I took it over. Its rent stabilized so they can't raise the rent any more than when my grandmother was alive. She and my grandfather lived here for over fifty years. On a teacher's salary that's the only way I can afford to live on Central Park West."

"I was going to ask you how you could afford to live here, but I thought it would be rude," Chemah said.

"You'd be surprised how many people inherit their apartments from parents and grandparents out here. I know some families who damn near go to war over who gets their grandparents' apartment."

A silence subtly settled between Nairobi and Chemah as they looked at each other. Nairobi inched closer to him. "Chemah, can I be totally honest with you?" Chemah nodded yes not knowing what she would say next. She began, "Like I told you in the car, when I meet someone whose vibe is on an even keel with mine, I make it my business to spend time with them. I don't want this to come out sounding like some line that I give every man I meet because I really don't. I mean I haven't been in a relationship in a long time. What I'm trying to say is I find myself very attracted to you. I feel a warmth from you that I don't normally feel from anyone when I first meet them. I'm not trying to scare you; I know we just met one hour ago, but I believe in love at first sight."

Chemah was startled by what she said, but he kept his composure. "I'm feeling you too, Nairobi; I just don't know if it's love right now." In actuality, Chemah knew it was love the moment she got into his car. He was fighting it with every bit of his mother's anti-white rationale. She had told him on more than one occasion, there's only one thing a white woman wants a black man for. Nairobi took his hand in hers. He could feel the softness and firmness of them.

"I'm not telling you my feelings to obligate you, Chemah," she said. "I just felt that some part of you was not allowing you to pursue me; and I just wanted you to know that I'm yours if you want me."

"Just like that, if I want you I can have you?" Chemah felt a wave of pleasure wash over him like the first time he'd held a girl's hand. He felt those unusual butterflies he got when he was twelve years old and he'd first told a girl he loved her. His mother had called it puppy love. "Nairobi, I haven't even kissed you yet."

"If you kiss me do you think it will change the way, you feel about me?"

"I don't know."

"Then kiss me and find out."

"That won't prove anything," he said. "How can you know in so short a period of time that you're in love in with someone?"

Nairobi leaned back, and away from him putting her hand behind the couch for support. "I know because I've been waiting to feel like this for a long time. I've never felt it before so it must be love," she answered.

Chemah thought he'd throw her a curve ball when he asked, "How many Black men have you been with?" It was always a possibility that she just had jungle fever.

"I've never been with a Black man," she said matter-of-factly. "Chemah, maybe I've taken the wrong approach. Why don't we just relax and drink our wine, and you can tell me more about yourself." This line of conversation was easier for him to get into, but immediately left him wanting that feeling he felt when she was expressing her feelings for him.

Chemah started by telling her he was one of three sons; the middle child. He told her his educational background, and how he had gone about getting a master's degree in forensic science and his job in a forensics lab. He even told her of his aspirations to work for the NYPD. They traded stories most of the evening; not thinking or even feeling the need for sustenance other than each other's company. When Chemah finally looked at his watch it was one-fifteen a.m. "I think it might be time for me to go," he said reluctantly.

"What time is it?"

"One-fifteen a.m."

"You could spend the night if you want. No strings attached."

"You know that's the same line I used on girls in college."

"It's not a line; you can sleep on the couch if you'd like. I just want to know that you're near me." The butterflies in his stomach were coming back; he was really feeling her now.

"Which way is the bedroom?" Chemah asked as he stood. Nairobi took his hand in hers and guided him down another hall to her bedroom. The bedroom was almost as big as her living room. Its space was not minimized by the few items she had in it: a king-sized bed with matching Ralph Lauren sheets and comforter (he had the same ones on his bed); a massage table next to the window facing the park; and a desk with a computer in the corner. The place was so immaculate it seemed she didn't use the room at all.

"We may have one problem," Chemah said. "I sleep in the nude."

"It's not a problem for me if it's not a problem for you. I sleep in the nude, too," she said.

"Are you trying to make me think that the two of us are going to be nude in this bed and nothing is going to happen?"

"I didn't say nothing was going to happen. No strings attached."

She shrugged her shoulders and pulled at his belt. Chemah took this as a cue that they would be undressing each other. He reached for the string on her sweatpants, but was intercepted by Nairobi's swift moving hands. She pushed his hands back to his sides, and as he was about to object, she put her index finger to his lips signaling for him to be quiet. Nairobi's eyes never lost contact with his as his pants fell to his ankles. Nairobi held his hips briefly and began lowering herself using first his hips, then his thighs to steady herself as she slowly descended to her knees. Chemah almost broke his silence to tell her that he didn't wear underwear but thought maybe she'd already figured it out. As she reached eye level with his penis, she broke eye contact with his eyes and stared admiringly at what he had to offer.

Chemah's excitement was becoming obvious; he started to thicken and lengthen right in front of her face, but all she did was stare. After a few moments of staring at his privates, her eyes and hands went to his feet. Undoing the bow in his laces she helped him take his shoes and socks off one after the other. She was then able to gently remove the remainder of his pants from around his ankles. Nairobi got off her knees with no help from him, and walked to the massage table neatly placing the pants on the table and the shoes and socks under it. Chemah felt silly standing there with nothing on but his Coogi sweater, so he pulled it off before she could turn back to him.

Nairobi turned toward him again and pouted as he extended his hand to her with the sweater in it. "I wanted to take that off you," she said. "I've been thinking about it since I first saw you this afternoon."

"So it's just been my body all along?"

"Noooo, it's just that you're so beautiful I wanted to unveil all of you myself," she replied.

"Well, when do I get to unveil you?"

"You don't," Nairobi said as she reached the wall and turned out the lights.

"I don't, huh," Chemah said, reaching for her in the dark, and missing. As his eyes adjusted to the darkness, he could make out Nairobi slipping into bed and out of his reach. Chemah carefully made his way to the bed and found his way under the sheets next to Nairobi. He felt for some part of Nairobi's body in the huge king-size bed, and found her hand. Chemah squeezed it gently and simultaneously pulled her to him as he pushed his body forward to meet hers. His eyes had fully adjusted to the darkness and he could see Nairobi's face by the moonlight coming through the window.

Chemah bent to kiss her and as their lips touched, her tongue entered his mouth searching for something soft and moist. Their tongues slipped in and out of each other's mouths as their kissing became more and more frantic. When he thought he couldn't take it anymore, he reached for the string on her sweat pants and pulled it. Her pants were immediately loose and he slipped his hand inside to touch her. Nairobi was very wet. Chemah easily entered her with a finger. Nairobi detached herself from his mouth and began kissing his neck as her breathing came harshly through clenched teeth. Chemah needed to gain more leverage to stimulate her with his hand, so he stopped touching her and used that same hand to tug her sweats off. As she felt him tugging, she lifted her hips off the mattress, and in one swift motion the pants were around her ankles. She kicked them off quickly; and he used that moment to tug her T-shirt over her head. Nairobi manipulated his penis in a jerky motion with her hand, as he kissed and licked her breast. Chemah slid his hand down her stomach to touch the moistness again. She caught his hand and guided it lower than he had intended to go.

"Get me ready, here," she said breathily, slipping his middle finger into her ass. Chemah had heard that some women preferred anal sex to vaginal sex, but he would have never guessed that Nairobi was one of those women. Either way as hard as she had gotten him, he wasn't going to argue. Chemah didn't know where she pulled it from, but he heard the tearing sound of a condom wrapper and the *thppt* sound you make spitting the remaining rapper from your mouth. Nairobi worked hard to put the condom over his penis as he continued to lave her breast and pump his finger into her ass using the vaginal juices that dripped out of her as a lubricant. Nairobi let him know she was ready to be entered by pulling him on top of her. Using his erection as a leash, she guided him to the space she wanted him to enter and pulled her legs far back so that her knees were against her shoulders.

Chemah had never had anal intercourse before, but like all men he fantasized about it many times. Initially, he was careful as he entered her, pulling back slowly, and entering her slowly again. Nairobi urged, "Do it harder, Chemah. Faster, faster. Oh God, make love to me." She grabbed a handful of his buttocks and pulled him into her. This kind of sex was everything he had imagined it to be. Raw and animalistic. Chemah came twice without ever getting soft or leaving her body. After the second time, he pulled out of her. Chemah was still rock hard. He knew it was the excitement of having fulfilled a fantasy and the newness of the relationship that was keeping him hard.

Chemah lay on his back trying to catch his breath. "Are you alright?" Nairobi asked, kissing his chest.

"Yeah, just give me a second to catch my breath, then you can show me to the shower."

"You're still hard," Nairobi noticed out loud.

"After I get out of the shower, we can make love again if you're not too tired."

"No, honey, I'm not tired; we can do it as many times as you like," Nairobi responded. She led him to the bathroom. He took a quick shower and came out ready to go again. This time he intended to make her come as fast as she had made him come. Chemah walked into the bedroom again and Nairobi was standing at the window staring out into the park. The room was still dark but he could see her silhouette against the light outside. She was still naked and looked beautiful. She had pulled her hair back so you could see her entire face.

Chemah came up behind her encircling her in his arms. "Hmmmm," she murmured, "that feels good," as he pressed his hardening penis against her backside. He turned her around to face him and saw tears forming in her eyes.

"What's wrong?" he asked. "Did I do something to hurt you?"

"No. You've been perfect from the moment I met you."

"Then why are you crying?" Chemah asked, not understanding her pain.

"Because I'm happy and I never want it to end."

"It doesn't have to end," Chemah said, lifting her into his arms and carrying her to the bed. This time he meant to make love to her slowly letting her know that his feelings for her were also very strong. They kissed each other ardently. Each touching and feeling the other with the intensity that is born with finding your soul mate.

"I'm a virgin," Nairobi said, unexpectedly breaking their kiss.

"Huh, what was that?" Chemah said stupidly.

"I AM A VIRGIN," Nairobi said, exaggerating each word.

Chemah stared at Nairobi through the darkness. "What are you talking about? We just got busy twenty minutes ago."

"We just had anal sex twenty minutes ago," she corrected him. "I've never been vaginally penetrated."

Chemah lay staring at her for a moment and then asked her the only question that came to his head. "Why?"

"Why am I a virgin or why do I have anal sex, or is your question why am I telling you now?" she said vehemently.

Chemah kept his composure. "Why don't you just tell me everything you want me to know on the subject of your virginity? If I have any questions when you finish I'll let you know."

"Well, it's very simple actually," Nairobi said. "My mother always told me that I should save my virginity for a special person. That person would be my husband. My mother's advice to me on my first date was that a boy would do anything he could to stick his penis into my vagina; so I should do everything that I could to not allow that to happen.

"My first date was John Delaney—blond hair, blue eyes, and a smile that broke through all my defenses," she continued. "I told John that I was saving my virginity for someone special, and John convinced me after a time that you didn't have to have vaginal sex to have fun. Sitting in my parents' living room watching TV after midnight on a Saturday, John and I started petting after my parents went to bed. John and my teenage insecurities convinced me that anal sex was okay. After all, Mom never said I shouldn't do it. Anyway he was the first, I enjoyed it, and all my other boyfriends since haven't complained when I offered them my buttocks in place of my vagina. I've since learned that almost all men fantasize about what I have always thought of as the natural thing to do. Including you," she said slyly.

"What do you mean, including me?" Chemah said, sitting up in her bed.

"Are you trying to say, you didn't enjoy the sex we just had?" Nairobi asked.

"I'm not saying I didn't enjoy it; I'm just saying that it's not my main concern when I'm having sex with a woman."

"And what is your main concern, Mr. Rivers?" Nairobi asked, reaching for his hand in the dark. Chemah was not ready to let Nairobi know all of his secrets yet. The white girl had him open, and she knew it. Chemah had to close the gap a little.

"I'm concerned about getting some sleep," he said, lying down and turning his back to her. Chemah could feel Nairobi smiling in the dark as she laid her arm over his body and ticked herself into the small of his back in spoon fashion. She softly kissed the back of his neck, and gave him one last squeeze before whispering a soft "good night" into his ear. He never fell asleep feeling that secure again.

Chemah awoke slowly feeling that he was still in the dream that he had just been disturbed from. He felt a soft moistness on his dick that was all too familiar. Raising himself onto his elbows he questioned the darkness. "What are you—" he started.

Nairobi continued to raise his nature with her mouth, but she gently urged him onto his back using her soft hands to put pressure on his chest. Her mouth never skipped a beat. Chemah could see through the window that the sun was starting to rise. The sky was a light purple, but it enabled him to see clearly in its glow. He looked down at Nairobi and saw that she was staring back at him. Her eyes dared him to try and hold back another orgasm. As his hips involuntarily began to jerk upward to meet Nairobi's mouth earnestly, she suddenly released him from her grip. The cool dawn air against his wet penis was uncomfortable enough to stop his orgasm. Chemah wasn't about to beg her to make him come, and he didn't have to. Nairobi kissed her way up his leg and on to his stomach, where she lingered to tongue his belly button. As she kissed her way up to his chest and then his neck, she simultaneously grabbed his dick. Chemah could feel the entrance to Nairobi's vagina dripping onto his hardness as she attempted to nestle the tip into her opening.

Chemah wanted to tell her she didn't have to do this. He wanted to tell her to save her virginity for someone who deserves her, but the only thing to come from his mouth was a breathless, "yessss." Chemah was in her raw dog (no condom, no contraceptives). It had been years since he made love to a woman without a condom, and the sensation that a woman's gripping vagina gives a man when it's skin to skin, almost made him weep.

He was concentrating on not cumming almost immediately after he was in her. She had already given him two orgasms and he didn't want to cum again until she got a few in herself. Whenever he felt himself about to blow, he would forcefully stop the thrust of her hips with his hands and go into a slower stroke that he could control. Chemah thought she had come as soon as she had impaled herself on him. She was shuddering and shaking as if she was having an epileptic attack, but he figured that was impossible. No woman comes that fast. They were both slippery with sweat and he couldn't hold it back any longer. Chemah felt his balls were about to crack open, they were so ready. "I can't hold it," he gasped.

"Give it to me, Chemah. Give me all of you. I'm cumming," Nairobi exalted. Chemah's cum blasted through him and into her when she made that announcement. They clung to one another, each riding out the other's orgasm. "Are you alright?" Nairobi asked as they lay holding each other.

"Shouldn't I be asking you that question?"

Nairobi smiled. "I'm happy."

"You're not in any pain, are you?"

"Shouldn't you have asked me that question two hours ago?" she said, raising her eyebrows.

"I'm sorry."

She one-upped him. "I love you." They both drifted to sleep lazily lying in each other's arms.

Chapter 6
WILL YOU STILL CALL ME SUPERMAN?

Margarita began working the room the minute she passed through the double doors of Sylvia's restaurant. She had been there before when other politicos decided they wanted to show they still had roots in the community. As a consultant, it was mandatory that she attend these functions. She was good at these sorts of social events. Her charm enabled her to move through a crowded room and make everyone feel as if she were paying special attention to them. *This evening will be different,* she thought. *Tonight, I'm concentrating on one man.*

As she eased through the crowded venue, she stopped for short periods to acknowledge men and women she had worked with and for on different occasions. Ignoring prospective clients would hurt business. People of power expected a certain amount of celebrity and when they didn't get it, they could be as vindictive as any scorned lover.

Margarita was talking to a city councilman when she noticed Chemah entering the room. It seemed to her that he filled the whole room with his presence. Her first impulse was to leave the councilman and introduce herself to Chemah. Instead she hung back feigning interest in every word that the councilman spoke, when in actuality she was tracking Chemah's every movement. She noted everyone he spoke to and how they reacted toward him. So far he hadn't spoken to anyone of importance, only line workers and some wannabe players.

Every woman he passed turned to look at him. The women who were already talking to men tried to do it inconspicuously, while the women who were alone blatantly stared. It wasn't that there weren't any other good-looking men in the room; on the contrary the room was loaded with fine men. It was obvious that Chemah was *The Man,* among these men. He walked gracefully and yet power-fully through the room. He didn't seem to notice the stares he received from women and men alike. His dreadlocks fell loosely about his shoulders. It was a significant contrast to the other men in the room; most wore low fades, or the shaved head that Michael Jordan had made fashionably acceptable. He was immaculately dressed from head to toe. It was obvious that his suit was tailored to fit perfectly, only an Armani suit fits like that; definitely Black Diamond.

Chemah had been in Sylvia's for thirty minutes already and Margarita could not foresee how she would meet him other than walking right up to him and introducing herself. Chemah was getting himself a drink at the bar when Margarita realized this was the first time he was alone since he'd entered. If she had to intro-duce herself, this was the perfect time. "Excuse me, councilman," she said. "I just saw someone that I have some pressing business with."

"Okay, dear, but hurry back. I have some ideas I wanted to pass by you," the councilman said.

As Margarita took her time sauntering toward Chemah, Khadijah Saeed walked right up to him and kissed him on the cheek. Although it was only a friendly hello kiss, it made Margarita flush with jealousy. She changed her gait and her demeanor to those of business without missing a stride as she approached the two friends. "Hey, Khadijah." Margarita leaned toward her friend and colleague for a perfunctory kiss on the cheek. "I just came over to make sure you went over those stats I sent you the other day. Your opponent, Mr. Rangel, is very familiar with this material and you did hire me to make sure you know what he knows."

"I did go over them, and I do have some questions about them, but now is not the time. Tonight we're here to make new alliances, raise some money, and have some fun; in that order." As if coming out of a reverie, Khadijah looked alter-nately at her two friends and smiled. "Do you two know each other?" Khadijah asked. Chemah and Margarita shook their heads no in unison. "Well, let's not stand on formalities. Margarita, this is Chemah Rivers. Chemah, I'd like you to meet my good friend and campaign manager, Margarita Smith."

"Pleased to meet you, Chemah." Margarita extended her hand to shake his. She felt both strength and tenderness in this first touch from him, and wondered what, if any, characteristics of her personality he garnered from touching her for the first time. A smirk played on Chemah's lips as he released Margarita's hand. "Is something wrong?" Margarita asked defensively.

"Pardon me?" Chemah queried.

"I said is something wrong?" Margarita repeated.

"I'm sorry; it's just that you're probably the first person in about two years that has pronounced my name right on the first try. Actually, I'm kind of impressed."

"Well, as long as you two are getting along swimmingly, I think I'll go tend to some of my other guests," Khadijah said. "Margarita, keep an eye on him. There are some other people I want him to meet, and he'll just disappear if you leave him alone for one second."

"Go ahead and do your thing, Miss Thang. I'll hold the fort down here." Margarita mocked a salute, and Khadijah returned it with both hands, as they both laughed.

Always the consummate professional, Khadijah adjusted her clothing before turning away from her two friends and changed her expression to one of polite humbleness before returning to the role of hostess for her constituents. Her two friends watched her as she started to make her rounds. Khadijah whispered into one gentleman's ear, receiving a smile in return. As she turned, she bumped into an elderly gray-haired woman, hugged and thanked her for coming all in one motion.

Margarita and Chemah turned their attention back to one another. "You know, I almost had the privilege of meeting you a few days ago," Margarita announced.

"Oh, when was this? I think I would've remembered you if we were ever in the same room before."

"Well, we weren't in a room together; it was more like an auditorium. Khadijah took me to your fifth-degree promotion the other day. It was quite impressive."

Chemah stared at her for a moment and realized that he did remember seeing her sitting near Khadijah at the promotion. "Ah, now I remember you. You had your hair down around your shoulders that day," he said, allowing her image at the promotion to cross his mind. Margarita attempted to hide her excitement knowing that he recognized her from that one occasion. She didn't want to let the opportunity pass. She thought she'd push her luck and explain how she came to be at his promotion.

"The other day Khadijah dragged me along to a ceremony a friend of hers was participating in. She insisted that she had to attend." Chemah blanched when the words "dragged me along" came out of Margarita's mouth. The look didn't go unnoticed by Margarita and she tried to clean it up. "I have to admit I've never been to an event like that and didn't know what to expect, but after I saw you I was very impressed. As I said I really wasn't that alert when she first mentioned your name to me; later I was too embarrassed to ask her what your name was. I hate to admit it but I did ask a few other people at the event your name. Don't tell her I told you that," she said in a conspiratorial tone. "On the way out I asked a couple of strangers if they knew your name. All they knew was that some people called you the 'Dragon of Harlem.'"

Chemah winced and put both hands up as if warding off an invisible opponent when he heard her use that moniker. "Shhhh, not so loud," he said in an exaggerated whisper.

"I'm sorry; does it bother you when people call you that?" Margarita asked.

"To be honest with you," Chemah admitted, "it was a name that the kids in my neighborhood used to tease me when I was growing up. I used to practice martial arts so much they used to say, 'Who do you think you are, Bruce Lee?' One kid said, 'Yeah, he thinks he's the 'Dragon of Harlem.' It stuck. After a while, when I became a black belt, it became a title of respect. But hardly anyone calls me that since I stopped competing in the tournament circuit."

"If you don't mind me asking, why did you stop competing? The way I heard everyone talk about you at the black belt promotional ceremony the other day, it was like you were unbeatable."

"I wouldn't say I was *unbeatable*. I've taken a few beatings in my day," Chemah admitted.

"I bet you're just being modest, Chemah," Margarita said, stroking his ego. "Well, if you're not doing tournaments anymore, what are you doing?"

"I just finished my master's degree at John Jay College in forensic science," Chemah informed.

"Forensic science? Do you mean like *Quincy*, the TV show?" Margarita was deliberately trying to sound like a dumb blonde.

"Yeah, crime scene technology is now the love of my life."

"You mean you want to do the same thing Oscar Madison does?" Margarita was pushing it.

Chemah laughed. "I know what you mean. Jack Klugman will always be Oscar Madison to me, too." Chemah brightened at the opportunity to talk about his plans for the future. "To be totally honest with you, I don't really want to be stuck in a laboratory slaving over test tubes all day. My real dream is to be a police detective," he said with the deepest sincerity.

"Well, did you take the police officer's exam?" Margarita asked, determined to find out as much as she could about Chemah.

"I sure did," Chemah said proudly. "I ranked number two on the written test out of ten-thousand applicants."

"Number two," Margarita repeated incredulously. "Don't they take you into the academy immediately when you rank that high?"

"Normally I think that they would but when I went down for my first interview and medical, they made a big deal out of an old knee injury that I had, and placed me on what they call medical review status. They've been making me jump through hoops bringing in documentation and medical reports from all sorts of doctors to verify that my knee is one hundred percent. They claim they don't want me to be a liability to the department, but I get the impression that my locks and color of my skin were more an issue that anything else," he said.

"Do you know that the only Black person that I saw in my first interview was a female sergeant? She was supposed to be in charge of the whole process, but after she introduced herself and gave the first instructions, she disappeared, and I haven't seen another colored face since. I know other applicants who are in the process and they tell me they have seen a few Black applicant investigators. Maybe I'm just paranoid but it feels like they're trying to stop a brother from getting a job."

Margarita smiled at his attempt to do a ghetto-brother imitation. "I'm sure you'll get in. You seem like the type of person that doesn't take no for an answer."

Chemah liked that she had confidence in him. "Thank you," he said, accepting her compliment. He looked at his watch. "Listen, I didn't realize it was getting so late. Khadijah seems to be engrossed in a lively discussion right now," he said, gesturing toward the hostess who now had the attention of five gray-haired men sitting apart from the rest of her guests. "Will you tell her that I had to leave and give her my deepest apologies for not being able to stay longer?" Chemah requested.

"Khadijah is going to be awfully disappointed that you left. You heard her say that she had some other people she wants to introduce you to," Margarita said, trying to postpone his departure.

"I know," Chemah said, "but I made other plans and I didn't realize it was this late."

"Well, if I can't convince you to stay, then at least let me escort you to your car," Margarita suggested. "Khadijah just wouldn't forgive me if I didn't extend you every courtesy her office has to offer." Margarita feigned subservience. "I wouldn't want to insult Khadijah's hospitality."

Chemah noticed the firm grip that Margarita had on his arm. As she led him toward the door, heads turned to look at what would appear to be the perfect couple. They were an ideal physical match in every way. His peanut-butter complexion mixed nicely with her chocolate-toned dermis. Her sinewy and curvaceous body almost clung to his muscular tall frame. Margarita was well aware of the powerful image they projected walking together and knew that only a man who commanded this much power and attention could ever gain her complete allegiance. The spring night air on Lenox Avenue was no relief from the noise and crowding in Sylvia's restaurant, as the sidewalks on Lenox Avenue were as busy and full of transactions as a Wall Street trading floor.

"How far away is your car?" Margarita asked.

"Right around the corner on One-Hundred Twenty-eighth Street. It's really not necessary for you to walk me, you know," he conceded.

"I know. But it'll give me a chance to see what kind of car you drive."

"Oh, so you're all about the Benjamins," Chemah chided.

Margarita chuckled. "Don't get it twisted, Mr. Dragon. I have my own money. I just find that you can tell a lot about a man from the kind of car he drives and how he maintains it. As a matter of reference, I'd say most women are wrong looking at a man's shoe size," she said as they got closer to his vehicle. "A car tends to be a more accurate indicator of what he's holding downstairs."

Chemah was almost impressed by Margarita's innuendos; he was not used to sisters who were this open discussing their sexuality.

"This is me," Chemah said, pointing to the car they had just stopped in front of. "Well, what's the verdict?"

"Hmmm, let me see, sedan, foreign, very sporty yet not ostentatious, clean lines. Immaculate interior. No extras. I'd say you're…Whoa, wait a minute. Is that a Blaupunkt system with Bose speakers? Initially, I would have said you're safe, reliable, and midsized." Margarita cleared her throat. She leaned in to stand toe to toe with Chemah as she stared directly into his eyes. "But now I'd have to say you like to 'make some noise.'"

"You could be right," Chemah said, breaking away from her gaze and opening the car door. "But I'll never tell."

Margarita was taken aback that he did not respond to her advances as she had expected. She quickly assessed the situation and tried another approach. "Well, can I get a ride?"

"Pardon me," Chemah said, catching the dual implication of her words.

"Back to Sylvia's. I know you're not going to just leave a sister standing out here," she said with her hands on her hips.

"I'm sorry," Chemah began. "I just thought—"

"I know what you thought," she snapped, cutting him off. "You thought I was asking for some other kind of ride."

"You have to admit," Chemah said, "you are sort of forward."

"Yes, I am forward," Margarita said, softening her voice as she opened the car door, "but I do not beg."

They drove quietly around the block heading back to Sylvia's, both wondering what to say before they went their separate ways.

Chemah wanted to apologize for assuming that she was coming on to him. He was attracted to her, but felt as if he were cheating on Nairobi. He rationalized to himself that he had just met Nairobi and the feeling that he had was just fleeting. Margarita was sensual in a way that Nairobi could never hope to be. *This is a motivated Black woman. I need to stick to my own kind,* he thought.

"Oh my God," Margarita exclaimed, breaking through Chemah's thoughts. "That's Congressman Jacobs."

"Where?" Chemah asked, startled out of his reverie.

"Behind us!" Margarita shouted, turning in her seat to look over the headrest. "Those boys are going through his pockets."

Chemah stopped the car abruptly and jumped out to find that the congressman and his assailants were fifty yards away on the curb to his left. Walking calmly, but swiftly toward what he knew would be a fight, Chemah breathed deeply, collecting the life energy surrounding all living things known as Chi. As he finally reached the congressman, Chemah assessed the situation. There were three teenagers approximately eighteen years old, two of whom were on either side, holding him under his arm pits making sure he couldn't move. The third kid was directly in front of the congressman. He held a box cutter low on the side of his leg so as not to be visible to passersby.

Chemah was aware of the damage a razor could do to the human body, and wanted to get between it and the congressman as quickly as possible. "My man," Chemah spoke directly to the brother holding the box cutter, "do you know who you're holding here?"

"Keep walkin' and mind your mothafuckin' business, Dread," the teenager with the box cutter responded. Chemah had seen the look on this young man's face before. He had gotten the money he was after, but he had to do something crazy to maintain his stature as a crazy motherfucker, not to be fucked with. He knew the congressman was about to be cut. Chemah grabbed the congressman by the back of his collar and backward off his feet, just as the blade made an arc past the front of his face. It only missed by a fraction of an inch, but it gave Chemah sufficient time and space to make sure there wouldn't be a second attempt. The two other thugs holding the congressman were forced to decide whether to hold on or fall with the congressman when he was yanked; they had opted to let go. Chemah was already moving swiftly. The one with the box cutter was holding it as if he were about to cut a steak. It was obvious he knew nothing about knife fighting, Chemah reasoned, or he might already have been cut.

As the blade made its second arc toward Chemah, he calmly stepped to his left and let it pass harmlessly past his right shoulder. In the same movement, Chemah's left hand moved in whiplike fashion to back fist the nose of the thug on his left who had regained his balance and attempted to throw a punch at Chemah's head. The thug's nose made a sickening crunching noise as the third knuckle in Chemah's fist found its target causing the cartilage in the bridge of his nose to protrude from its skin. The wildly swinging momentum of the box cutter carried the danger of the blade to the left. Using a triangle foot pattern Chemah immediately stepped forward with his right foot, which caused him to be directly behind the young man with the box cutter. Before the brother could regain his balance, Chemah's outstretched fingers had found his trachea with an eagle claw grip. Chemah used the weight of the young man's off-balance body to allow the thug to feel the extent of the grip that Chemah purchased on his throat before pulling him erect by the sheer force of his fingers.

"Drop the blade," Chemah whispered dangerously into his ear. He squeezed his fingers an extra fraction of an inch into his throat for incentive. The blade fell impotently from the thug's hand onto the curb. The third thug eyed Chemah nervously looking alternately from the congressman back to Chemah as if trying to decide what to do next.

"Yeah, what you gonna do now?" came a lazy drawl from the doorway of the building they were in front of. Chemah instinctively tightened his grip on the throat of the thug before turning quickly to direct his attention toward the new threat.

Chemah eased up when he recognized who it was. Andre McCullough hopped lightly off the stoop of the building and faced the third thug. The thug seemed to recognize Andre, too, and now blinked nervously as he looked from Andre to Chemah. "My suggestion to you," Andre said, stepping to the thug, and prodding him in the forehead with his index finger to emphasize his words, "is that you unball your punk-ass fist, apologize to these people for being stupid enough to stick somebody on my block, then take your sorry-ass boy to the hospital and see if they can do something about fixin' his grill." The young man nodded his head zealously, but as he attempted to walk by Andre, he was stopped. "And take this motherfucker with you, too," Andre said, pointing to the teenager Chemah still had in a steel grip. "Let him go," Andre said authoritatively. Chemah released his grip and pushed the thug away in one motion.

The young thug turned back to Chemah. "I'ma see you, motherfucker; you don't know who you just fucked with," he threatened.

Andre snatched the unsuspecting thug off his feet and held him up against the building. The young man once again found himself being held by his throat. This time his feet were dangling under him, as he was choked. Andre talked calmly. "You know who I am?" The thug attempted to nod. "Good. That man you just threatened, that's my family. You threaten him; that means you're threatening me. You're not threatening me, are you?" Andre asked with fire in his eyes. The thug attempted to shake his head no this time. "Good," Andre said, allowing the thug to fall at his feet. "Now get the fuck out of here before I change my mind, and do you something." Andre turned away from the crumpled young man as a sign that he was being allowed to leave.

Margarita was already on the scene helping the congressman dust himself off and compose himself.

"I see you haven't changed any," Andre said to Chemah with a chuckle. The two men hugged each other in a genuine show of affection. "Still saving lives, I see." Andre laughed.

"Well, it seems like you're the one that saved my life this time," Chemah retorted.

"Saved your life?" Andre mocked him. "Shit, I knew what you was gonna do to them dudes. I was scared of what they were gonna look like when you finished." He laughed. "Them motherfuckers need to be thanking me for saving their lives." Andre looked over his shoulder at the congressman. "He a friend of yours?" he asked, motioning with his head. Chemah nodded. "Yeah, well the 'Dragon' needs to tell his friends to keep off these unfriendly streets when the sun goes down," Andre chided him.

"Well, if Droopy had a tighter leash on his dogs, decent people would be able to walk the street," Chemah chided back.

"Droopy? Who the fuck you calling Droopy?" Andre laughed. "Man, ain't nobody called me Droopy since I was fourteen years old! Man, wasn't it you that gave me that name?"

"That's right! But you're the one that started calling me Dragon. At least nobody calls you Droopy anymore."

"Well, shit all you gotta do is kill a few people," Andre said matter-of-factly. "After that, niggas will call you whatever you tell them to." He laughed. Andre's demeanor changed abruptly. "Yo, I don't have to tell you this episode don't go no further than this, Chemah."

"I've got no problem with that," said Chemah, "but I'm not the one that was attacked." Both Andre and Chemah turned to face the congressman and Margarita who were engaged in their own conversation. "Are you alright, sir?" Chemah asked.

The congressman turned to him. "I'm fine. I want to thank you for your help, young man. You know thirty years ago I was a damn good fighter myself. Those punks wouldn't have stood a chance against me back then." Chemah and Andre both nodded respectfully as the elder man spoke of his youth. "Then again, thirty years ago a black man wouldn't have attacked another black man in Harlem for no reason. We had some cohesion. The Black Panthers and the Nation of Islam were around. I never did agree with much of what either of those groups were doing, but I'll tell you one thing; if an old man got attacked on Harlem's streets, you could bet your ass they'd have done something about it."

Chemah interrupted him. "Sir, if it's okay with you, I think it would be a good idea if we didn't involve the police in this," he said, glancing at Andre.

"No, no, no, no police," said the congressman. "That's all I need," he grumbled. "If the newspapers get a hold of this, they'll just make more of it than it is. They're already on me about some misappropriation of funds. I've tried to explain to them that my campaign extended too—"

Margarita interrupted him before he could finish his sentence. "Congressman, I think we should get away from here right now." She took his arm and led him away.

The congressman turned back to Chemah. "If there's ever anything I could do for you, young man, call my office." The congressman shook Chemah's hand. "You, too," he said, shaking Andre's hand as an afterthought.

"Chemah, I'll call you," Margarita called over her shoulder as she again led the congressman away.

Andre turned to Chemah. "I'll check you later, man," he said, giving Chemah dap. "And tell your mom I said hi," Andre added as he turned into the building. "I know she still loves me." In fact, Chemah's mother had always been fond of Andre. She had refused to call him "Droopy" when everyone else did and had once confided to Chemah that Andre was the only one of his friends worth a lick.

"I'll let her know you're still alive," Chemah said, but he was talking to himself. Dre was already gone and the sidewalk was empty. Chemah wondered if it was too late to call Nairobi as he started his car.

Chapter 7
GOOD NEWS AIN'T ALWAYS GOOD NEWS

Chemah's phone was now ringing for the sixth time. He had not gotten any sleep the night before. Nairobi's mom had had a heart attack and he had waited in the airport with her for three hours on standby for a flight to Florida. He knew he should have gone straight home after the episode at Sylvia's.

Chemah was wondering why his answering machine wasn't picking up, and was suddenly startled by his own voice. *Hi, you've reached the home of Chemah Rivers. I can't come to the phone right now so leave the digits. Peace.* Beep.

Damn, I sound corny, Chemah thought, making a mental note to change the message on his machine.

Hi, Chemah, this is Margarita. I just called to give you some good news.

Chemah lunged at his phone when he heard Margarita's voice. "Hello, hello," he said, attempting to sound sleepy.

"Well hell is low." Margarita laughed. "I see you screen your phone calls. Is that so that all those sisters that are tracking you down can't get their claws into you?" she teased.

"Sisters, shoot. Most sisters don't pay me any mind at all."

Margarita was only now realizing how oblivious Chemah was to his own good looks. "Do you mean to tell me you don't notice all the women that stare at you when you walk down the street?"

"You know it's funny you say that. It just so happens sometimes when I think a woman is looking at me. I try to make eye contact back with them, but when I turn to look at them, they turn away and ignore me," Chemah explained.

Margarita knew it was the low self-esteem of women who thought they couldn't attract such a good-looking man that made them look away. But she wouldn't give Chemah that bit of insight. "Well, I would never turn away from you." There was an uncomfortable silence on Chemah's side of the line. "Are you always going to disrespect me when I try to flirt with you?" Margarita exclaimed, feigning exasperation.

"I'm sorry, Margarita. I didn't mean to dis you. I was just digesting what you were saying. I know that you like me; it's just that I really started seeing someone recently, and I don't really know where it's going."

Margarita was taken aback by this information. She had never considered that he was already interested in someone else. "Well, far be it from me to try to take you away from the woman you love," Margarita prodded.

"Who said anything about love?" Chemah defended himself.

"Well, then if you're not in love, what's wrong with liking more than one person?" Margarita asked. Chemah was slow to respond. "Well!" Margarita insisted.

"Nothing, I guess," Chemah said hesitantly. "I thought most women were against guys seeing more than one woman at a time."

Margarita was at her best when she had to think fast. "I'm not 'most women,'" she said quickly, "and furthermore, you probably wouldn't be able to appreciate me if you didn't have someone to compare me to."

"Are you saying you believe you can be measured against any woman?" Chemah challenged her.

"No, I believe that any woman will fall short when compared to me," Margarita said with confidence.

"Don't you think that sounds a little conceited?"

"No, I don't. And I won't say that I'm convinced either." Margarita continued, "But I do think you'd be convinced if you'd open up and give us a chance to get to know one another." There was another pause of silence on Chemah's line.

"Just something for you to consider," Margarita said offhandedly. "Now, back to business. How would you like to be in the next police academy class, which by the way begins in three days?"

Chemah's attention was immediately rapt. "What do you mean?"

"I've spent all morning in a certain congressman's office, explaining to him how a certain man who saved his life last night was being kept out of his chosen profession. A few well-placed phone calls later, and we got you into the next class."

"Are you kidding me?" Chemah said excitedly.

"No, I'm not kidding. As a matter of fact, I had them fax over to my office the remaining papers that you have to fill out, and once we fax them back, it's a done deal. You will be officially sworn in in three days."

"Forgive me for being so suspicious, Margarita, but to what do I owe this huge favor that you're doing for me?"

"You don't owe me anything," Margarita said indignantly. "I saw you perform a selfless act last night that made me say; 'This brother deserves to be a member of the NYPD.' I'd do the same thing for anybody else that reacted the way you did in that incident last night. Don't you think you deserve it?"

"Of course, I think I deserve it. I'm just in shock. Well, I'm glad you believe in yourself because I think a lot of good things are going to be happening for you," Margarita predicted.

"I don't know what could happen that could be as good as this."

"I think taking a beautiful Black woman to lunch could be a start," Margarita responded.

"And where would I find this beautiful Black woman?" Chemah played along.

"As luck would have it, Chemah, I just happen to be such a beautiful and hungry black woman."

"I guess you'll do," Chemah said jokingly. "Where should we meet?"

"I'll pick you up in thirty minutes.".

"OK," Chemah said hesitantly. "Let me give you my address."

"I already know where you live."

Chemah was surprised. "How do you know that?"

"A lady mustn't tell all of her secrets," Margarita responded. It had just dawned on Chemah that he hadn't given her his phone number either, but here she was talking to him on the phone. "See you in thirty minutes," Margarita finally said.

"I'll be ready and waiting. Goodbye."

Chapter 8
Who says I'm dumb!

Chemah wanted to share the news with Nairobi but he hadn't remembered to ask the number to where she was staying. He was in a mood to celebrate and sharing the afternoon with a beautiful woman was not a bad way to do so.

Chemah's shift didn't start until one p.m., but he had already decided he wasn't working today. He called in and told his supervisor he wouldn't be in but would definitely see him tomorrow. He gave no other explanation. Chemah never took days off, and was never late, so his supervisor didn't question him this first time. Whatever was going on with Chemah, it must've been important. He didn't shirk his responsibilities at the job, and was well liked by everyone. He was considered to be a serious young man.

Chemah decided to dress up for his lunch date. He had recently purchased a powder-blue Sean John suit that he had not worn. He pulled it out of his closet, took the pants off the hanger, and laid them on the bed. He placed the jacket, still on the hanger, above the pants, and stepped back to admire the look. Chemah decided to make the outfit look less formal by adding a casual navy blue pair of Prada shoes and a white Calvin Klein button-down T-shirt to the ensemble. After getting out of the shower, Chemah put on his outfit and reflected on whether or not he should leave a message on Nairobi's answering machine. There was a chance she would call to check her messages. He could leave one that said to call his house and leave a forwarding number. As he touched the receiver, the phone rang and he picked up.

"Hey, sweetheart, I'm outside your door waiting for you. Don't keep me waiting too long."

"I'll be right out, Margarita," Chemah said.

He tossed the cordless phone onto the couch and went to the mirror to check himself one last time before stepping out the door. Chemah liked what he saw: a look of deep satisfaction.

He walked out of his apartment attempting to look subdued and mellow, but he felt like jumping into Margarita's car and kissing her for accomplishing what he himself had struggled to attain. Chemah opened the door to Margarita's Jaguar and sat in the plush tanned leather seat.

"So where are we off to?" Chemah said, facing Margarita.

She leaned over and kissed Chemah tenderly on the mouth. Caught by surprise, Chemah opened his mouth to protest, only to find that he had inadvertently given access to Margarita's soft and velvety tongue. Chemah couldn't help but respond to the delicious feel of her tongue in his mouth. Chemah allowed his tongue to dance with hers, as they took turns probing one another's mouths. Margarita finally broke the kiss and let out a breathless sigh.

"Hmmmm. Now, that wasn't so bad, was it?" she asked.

Chemah seemed to still be recovering from the kiss as he silently shook his head in response. Margarita turned her attention to the street she was on, putting her Jaguar into gear. She pulled out of the parking spot, simultaneously placing her light hand on Chemah's thigh.

"I've thought of the perfect place for us to celebrate," she said.

Chemah sunk into his seat allowing himself the luxury of having someone else take the reins for a while. Margarita sped along the street smiling to herself. She had taken Chemah's relaxation and silence as a sign of submission.

Chapter 9
LOVE HAS REPERCUSSIONS

It had been three months since Nairobi was in New York. She'd stayed in Florida the whole time her mother was sick. She had called back to her teaching job and had arranged to take a leave of absence until her mother was well. Her father and she had taken turns staying at her mother's bedside praying and consoling each other until the day her mother's health had taken a turn for the worse, and she flatlined during a cardiac episode.

Now she was trying to put the pieces of her life back together. Although she had requested a leave of absence, she had decided while in Florida that she wouldn't return to teaching. She'd have to start putting her resume out right away. What she thought about now was resuming her relationship with Chemah. She hadn't had time or the inclination to talk to him while her mother was sick, but now she was starved for affection, and she longed to see the man she loved. She wondered if he missed her as much as she missed him. His number was listed in the phone book; there was only one Chemah Rivers listed and she started to call as soon as she found the number.

Chemah picked up the phone on the second ring. "Hello."

"Hello, Chemah, it's me, Nairobi," she responded nervously.

Chemah didn't know what else to say, so he asked the obvious. "Where have you been? I tried calling."

Nairobi had no reasonable answer for him. She had been distraught at her mother's illness and had allowed all her other relationships to suffer.

"I want to see you," she said, changing the subject.

"I don't think that's such a good idea," Chemah said slowly. "I'm seeing someone else now."

"Someone else?" she asked in disbelief.

"I'm sorry, I haven't heard from you in three months. I figured you changed your number and moved away to get away from me."

"My mother was dying. I wasn't thinking of anything else." Nairobi could feel herself getting dizzy.

"I'm sorry to hear about your mother, Nairobi. I really am, but if you really cared about us you would have at least called to give me a number to reach you. How do you think I felt when day after day I waited for a phone call from you and got nothing?" Chemah's voice raised a few octaves.

"Please, Chemah, give me another chance," Nairobi pleaded.

"I'm sorry, Nairobi. I don't have another chance to give," Chemah said as he felt his own heart break for the second time in three months.

"Chemah, don't do this," Nairobi continued to plead.

"I didn't do this; you did, Nairobi."

Chemah hung up the phone and when it rang immediately again, he steeled his heart to stop himself from crying and letting his soul mate back into his life. When Chemah wouldn't pick up the phone again, Nairobi felt sick to her stomach. She had never vomited in her life but the pain she now felt made her lose her lunch. She would never call him again, she swore to herself. Two minutes later, she was dialing his phone number. This time when he wouldn't pick up, she felt faint. She decided to lie down thinking that when she awakened, everything would be well again. It took her two weeks to get the courage to call Chemah again. His phone number had been changed and unlisted. She almost lost her mind.

Chapter 10
MAY THE GOOD MAN FIND PEACE

Yesterday had been Chemah's sixth-year anniversary married to Margarita. They had a pleasant enough dinner at Fresco's Restaurant in Midtown Manhattan, both enjoying a lobster and steak dinner.

The past six years seemed to have gone by in the blink of an eye. Chemah had taken the sergeant's test in his second year, immediately after completing his probationary period with NYPD, and was promoted in his third year. He seemed to be on the fast track to success working for New York's finest. Chemah had made detective right before being promoted and had asked to stay on his assignment in homicide. Given his experience as a forensic scientist and the lack of forensic specialists in the force, his request had been granted.

Margarita had not been happy with his decision. She had wanted him to take an assignment sitting at a desk somewhere away from the streets. She fantasized that he would be chief of the department—someday maybe even commissioner. In the back of her mind, she knew he would never be happy at a desk job, but still she never relented asking him to let her use her contacts to get him an assignment off the streets.

By all rights, Chemah should have been one of the happiest men on earth. He had a beautiful wife. He lived in a beautiful five-story brownstone home. He had the job he had dreamed about since he was a little boy, and his wife and his combined income allowed them to purchase whatever their hearts desired. Although

Chemah always acknowledged and counted his blessings, he always felt that true happiness was always eluding him.

Something was missing in his life, and he could not figure out what it was. He had tried on several occasions to broach the subject of his discontent with his wife, only to have his feelings dismissed. Margarita's solution to Chemah's unhappiness was sex. Upon any mention of being unhappy Margarita would instigate a rigorous sexual encounter. These sessions would be marathonian, lasting three to four hours. Margarita would do anything to keep Chemah's attention. No sexual act was barred from their bedroom. The only two things that were consistent in their lovemaking was Margarita's penchant for prolonging him from cumming until she was ready to let him release. And that she always preferred to finish him off with her mouth.

Last night after dinner they had gone home and made love as usual. Chemah couldn't sleep after they had made love, feeling even less fulfilled than usual. Chemah had decided not to mention his decision to Margarita to return to the dojo. It had always been the one place where he was accepted for who he was. No one had ever tried to change him. Both his instructors, Grandmaster Sam McGee and Master Dwayne McGee, had been his surrogate fathers when his own dad couldn't be there for him. All of the senior students had treated him like their little brother when his big brother had gone off to college. And later he had considered so many other students his little brothers and sisters. He knew that it was the feeling of belonging to a family that he was missing. His mother and father had moved to Florida three years ago. Chemah visited when he could, but that was twice a year at the most.

Margarita had decided they would start having children the first year after they were married. After two years of unsuccessful attempts at having children, they went to a fertility doctor. Margarita and Chemah had both undergone tests to determine why they weren't successful. Initially, Chemah had protested. "Black folks don't go to fertility doctors. We just keep fucking until we get it right."

"Well, we've been fucking for two years and it has become apparent that you can't get it right," Margarita accused him.

Chemah eventually relented as he couldn't take Margarita's constant abuse. Chemah had left work early on Monday. He and Margarita had decided to meet at home at noon and drive to the fertility clinic.

Chemah got into the passenger side of Margarita's Jaguar. He knew it was futile to suggest he drive. Margarita preferred to drive whenever possible and Chemah knew above any other time, she needed to feel she was in control now. Chemah put his hand in her lap attempting to alleviate some of the tension between them. Margarita realized what he was trying to do and allowed one of her hands to come off the steering wheel to hold his hand. Margarita glanced over at him and squeezed his hand, signaling that she accepted his gesture of confused understanding.

They had arrived at the clinic in Elizabeth, New Jersey in record time. As they pulled into the parking lot, Margarita let go of his hand, enabling her to maneuver the Jaguar into the parking spot she had picked. Before they walked through the clinic's entrance, Chemah had taken Margarita's hand in his own once again. Margarita wasn't always comfortable with public shows of affection, but she understood that Chemah was trying to be supportive, and she didn't want him to think that she was unappreciative of his caring. She knew from experience that Chemah had a need to feel desired. He was used to being the person that saved the day, and she by her own definition was superwoman.

Margarita allowed Chemah to lead her into the clinic. They stopped at the reception desk to announce their arrival. Chemah had been prepared to fill out forms. He released Margarita's hand and picked up a clipboard with an application.

"That won't be necessary, Mr. Rivers," the receptionist said, holding out her hand to take the clipboard from Chemah. "Your wife has already taken care of all the paperwork through our website. Just have a seat in the lounge and a nurse will be right with you." The receptionist pointed to a door to the right of the desk, indicating they should go that direction. Margarita stepped through the door first, with Chemah following a step behind her. Margarita stopped abruptly, just inside the doorway. Chemah looked over Margarita's shoulder and smiled as he thought exactly what Margarita was thinking. There were five white couples waiting in the lounge area. Chemah smiled at Margarita. *Black people just fuck until they get it right.*

Margarita pursed her lips and sat down in the middle of the group. She said hello to everyone, and everyone responded with a simultaneous "hi." Chemah followed behind, waving a perfunctory hello. Once again the group said "hi" in unison. One by one each couple was led away by a nurse. Finally a nurse came to get Margarita and Chemah.

After a short meeting with the doctor to explain the procedures, Chemah and Margarita were led away to different parts of the clinic. Chemah was directed to a small room that housed a television, a VHS player, a bed, a table and chair, and a cabinet. Chemah was told that the cabinet was stocked with magazines and videos that he might find helpful in filling the specimen cup with semen. He had known all along what his part in the examination process would be, but he found these people to be so impersonal and casual about the subject that it put him off. He didn't believe he could produce under these kinds of conditions.

Chemah checked the cabinet to see what their pornography selection consisted of. There were ten tapes in the cabinet. They seemed to have one of everything: white-on-white sex, black-on-black sex, interracial sex, S&M sex, foot fetish sex, gay sex, lesbian sex, midget sex, and sex with pregnant women. It took him a minute before he decided. Chemah picked a video with Asian women. He had never dated an Asian woman and had never seen one naked. This seemed to be as good a time as any. After pushing the video into the machine and pressing play, Chemah hopped onto the bed to make himself comfortable.

The video started with two Oriental women going down on one another. Chemah found himself staring intently at a silky-haired vagina. Maybe he just hadn't been with enough women in his short lifetime, but he would swear that this was the prettiest pussy he had ever seen. It was bare of all hair on the sides. The sparse hair was right above the very beginning of the vagina itself. The hair was long, straight, and fine, like strands of silk. The lips of the pussy were pink and looked swollen and tender. What intrigued Chemah the most about this sight was the size of the smaller Asian girl's clitoris. It was the size of a grape. The way that the other Oriental girl was alternately sucking and licking it had made it engorge until it was purple.

After about thirty seconds of watching this performance, Chemah had his dick in his hand and was gliding up and down along the shaft in time with the laving that the bigger Oriental girl was giving the one with the enormous clit. Chemah's excitement grew with every lick that the bigger girl exacted on the smaller one. He used the juices coming out of the slit on the head of his dick to lubricate himself well. He used his thumb to smear the head with the sticky clear substance, which caused more copious amounts to ooze freely down the shaft. After a few minutes, his whole dick was glistening as if it radiated its own light. Chemah moved his hand faster and faster until he was almost ready to come. He listened to the labored breathing of the girl with the engorged clitoris and stared transfixed at the distorted grimace on her face.

When he heard her shout, "I'm cumming," he knew he was cumming, too. He sprayed the first wad of come over the bed sheet when he realized that he had not prepared for this moment. The sterile canister they had given him to fill was across the room on the table. Chemah attempted to hold the sperm back by gripping his dick even more tightly, but it just kept cumming, gob after gob until it was dribbling out of the head of his dick and onto his fist.

Chemah got up off the bed and walked toward the table with the sterile canister and tissues. He was embarrassed and chastised himself as he cleaned the mess he had made on the bed with the generic tissue that had been supplied. By the time he finished cleaning he was in much better humor. Chemah decided to try it again. This time he would be prepared. He brought the sterile canister and the tissue over to the bed. He smiled to himself as he looked through the selection of videos again. The S&M tape gravitated to his hand as if it knew it was his next choice. Chemah had always been curious about this form of sex. He was still smiling when he popped the tape into the video player.

"I'll fill that container if it takes me all day," he said out loud, plopped down on the bed, and pulled his dick out again.

It was five-thirty p.m. Margarita and Chemah were the only ones waiting in the lounge area of the clinic. It was costing Margarita a lot of extra money to get their results back immediately, but she couldn't take the strain of not knowing when she would be able to have a family of her own much longer.

Chemah had taken more than an hour to produce the sperm that was needed for his test. Margarita had known it would be hard for him to go into a room alone and produce the sperm sample. She knew her man; he just wasn't built like that. She had toyed with the idea of going into the room with him. She knew just how she would get that sample.

"You know we would already be finished here if you hadn't taken so long in that room," Margarita chastised.

"Hey, just be glad I came out at all," Chemah responded. "It could have taken a lot longer, you know."

Margarita looked at him fondly. "I'm sorry, honey," she apologized. I know how hard that must have been for you."

They waited another three minutes in silence before the nurse came to get them. "The doctor will see you now," she announced.

When the tests came back indicating that Margarita was barren she was inconsolable. Margarita didn't cry. She would not accept pity from the doctor, her friends, and especially not Chemah.

Chapter 11
NOT THE PRODIGAL SON

In the previous five years Margarita had concentrated on her work and on keeping Chemah happy. Now it just wasn't enough for Chemah anymore. He packed his *gi* and prepared to leave for the dojo. It was an approximate half-mile from his home to the dojo and Chemah hadn't taken the opportunity to visit in five and a half years. He was ashamed at his own disloyalty.

Chemah was getting dressed in the locker room with five other students who were late for the karate class. He didn't recognize any of them, and understood why three of them put on brown belts and two of them donned green belts. He had not been here in more than five years, and it took at least four years to earn a brown belt.

As Chemah walked up the stairs of the Hansborough Recreation Center, also known as the bathhouse, where the Harlem Goju Dojo had been located for the past twenty-five years, he anticipated that he would not know many of the students who now attended. As Chemah reached the doorway of the dojo, he bowed his greeting to the school. There were approximately eighty students at the school tonight. Chemah knew there were many more members of the school than were present at the class this evening. Like him, students left for months or years at a time, but always found their way back.

Chemah saw Grandmaster Sam McGee and Master Dwayne McGee at the center of the floor instructing a large group of pee wee (seven years and under) white belts. Chemah walked forward into the middle of the dojo. As he reached the group, all the white belts glanced at him. Both instructors followed their students' eyes and turned in one synchronized motion. Both instructors' eyes brightened significantly as Chemah bowed low to them to show his respect.

When Chemah stood up straight, Grandmaster spoke first. "I'm glad to see you back home," he said, taking him into his arms and hugging him in a show of genuine manly love.

When Grandmaster released him, Master Dwayne grabbed him in a bear hug that squeezed all of the air out of his lungs. He let Chemah back down onto the floor and immediately lit into him as if he had just seen him the day before.

"Your body feels soft," he said. "When was the last time you trained? Never mind," he said before Chemah could answer. "Take over these white belts. Maybe they'll remind you what training is all about."

Master Dwayne introduced Chemah to the young boys and girls, then he and Grandmaster walked away to inspect the other students' progress. Chemah started the pee-wee white belts with a set of push-ups. He made sure that he did all of the exercises right along with them. He tried to make each exercise fun. He knew that was the key to keeping the attention of children under seven years old. He tried to imitate some of the old games that Master Dwayne had used to keep his and hundreds of children's attention when practicing martial arts. The children took to him instantly. Then came the most serious part of the training—the kumite sparring. Chemah knew he could not allow them to take this part of the training lightly, but he did not want the children to try and hurt each other. He also knew that some children this age would want to quit because they would be afraid to be hit.

Chemah started by explaining how they would proceed in their training. "What we're going to do now is have a short round robin tournament. One point wins the match. That way everyone gets a chance to fight. If you win your match, you stay on the mat until someone beats you. Now, who's going to be first?"

A tall, dark-skinned boy raised his hand immediately.

"Come on up," Chemah said. "Who else wants to be first?"

No one else volunteered.

"How about you?" Chemah asked a curly-haired young boy who stood up front. Chemah had noticed the boy earlier in the lesson. He followed direction very well and his kata looked sharp.

"Alright, face each other and when I say 'fight,' you can kick or punch to the chest or stomach for a point. Do you both understand?" Chemah asked.

Both students nodded.

"Ready, fight!" Chemah announced. Both children started kicking each other simultaneously but none scored.

"Stop!" he shouted.

The students stopped immediately. "Alright, that was very good," Chemah said. "But you have to strike the torso to score a point. One more try. Ready, fight!"

The curly-haired boy punched straight at the bigger boy's chest. When the larger one realized he was about to lose, he struck the curly-haired boy in the face, knocking him to the floor. Chemah helped the curly-haired boy to his feet and wiped the single tear that had formed in his right eye. Chemah stood and addressed all of the white belts.

"We have a disqualification for illegal contact. Our winner," he proclaimed, pointing to the curly-haired boy. Chemah knew how important it was for the curly-haired boy to fight again immediately before he had time to think of being afraid.

"Who's next?" Chemah asked.

When no one answered, he picked a little girl who was slightly bigger than the curly-haired boy. Chemah gave them the rules again and allowed them to fight. The curly-haired boy did not seem afraid; he just kept punching until he scored a point. One after the other he continued to beat every opponent that Chemah put up against him. The little boy had no real skill, but the look of determination on his face made you feel like cheering him on. After the curly-haired boy beat his eighth opponent, Chemah had decided he had fought enough.

As he was about to ask him to sit down, Grandmaster Sam McGee appeared next to him. "Let him keep fighting," the Grandmaster said with a finality that Chemah knew better than to question.

The curly-haired boy continued beating his opponents until there was only one left. By that time, he was covered with sweat and breathing hard. Chemah was worried that he was overfatigued, but the Grandmaster did not seem moved. The curly-haired boy beat his final opponent which was another little boy of about the same age and height.

Grandmaster spoke again. "Let him fight his first opponent again."

Chemah gave Grandmaster a questioning look and received an unwavering glare in return. Chemah should have known better than to question the grandmaster's reasoning. Chemah called the tall dark-skinned boy again. The little boy jumped to his feet seemingly happy and ready to fight.

"Wipe that smile off of your face, young man. This is a fight, not a game," Grandmaster said.

Chemah gave instructions to both fighters but seemed to be directing them toward the taller of the two boys. "No facial contact; that means no punching to the face. When I say stop, stop immediately. Bow to me."

Both boys bent at the waist and bowed to Chemah.

"Bow to each other."

The boys mimicked what they had seen the older students doing, faced each other, bowed, and got into their respective fighting stances. They both looked like they had seen one too many episodes of either *Dragonball Z* or *Power Rangers*.

"Ready, fight," Chemah commanded.

Both boys attacked at the same time; the taller one attacked with a slow round house kicking which landed on the upper fleshy part of the smaller boy's arm. The curly-haired boy lunged forward and it was immediately evident what he was attempting to do He threw a straight punch with his right hand aiming directly at the bigger boy's face. The curly-haired boy missed his target, but continued to throw punches aimed at the bigger boy's face.

"Stop," Chemah commanded, but his commands appeared to have fallen on deaf ears.

The smaller boy continued punching, and the bigger boy threw another kick with the same leg, this time connecting with the smaller boy's hip. This didn't seem to faze the smaller boy who had finally been able to reach his target and struck the taller boy in the face. Chemah reached out and grabbed him by the back of his *gi*. The little boy's punch didn't have enough force to do any damage to the bigger child, but the act of actually having punched him seemed to have a calming effect on him. Chemah could feel the smaller boy's body slump in his arms. It was now evident to Chemah that the little boy's body had been tense as a coil since he had been hit in the face earlier. Chemah ordered both boys to stand before him.

"I said no striking to the face," he spoke to the smaller boy. "Now shake hands and both of you sit down." Both boys shook hands, smiled, and ran to sit.

Grandmaster Sam McGee clapped his hands three times, which was the signal for the entire class to come to order. All of the students knew what to do. They formed eight lines, according to rank, and stood straight, looking directly ahead. Even the smallest five-year-old white belt knew his place. Seven other instructors with the rank of third-degree black belt or above stood at the front of the class with Grandmaster Sam and Master Dwayne. Grandmaster addressed the class, going over the lessons of the day, and then Master Dwayne took over, telling all the students what was expected of them before dismissing the class.

When the class was over, the dojo floor filled with parents retrieving their children. Chemah took this opportunity to talk to Grandmaster Sam. "Grandmaster, why did you allow that boy to continue fighting?" he asked in his most humble tone, knowing Grandmaster did not like being questioned.

The Grandmaster answered succinctly, "I know why you allowed him to continue fighting, Chemah. You believed that he had to get right back up on that horse so that he would never be afraid, isn't that right?" Chemah nodded in agreement. "But I know the spirit of all my students, Chemah. That little boy was never scared, he needed closure. He knows that the other boy is bigger and stronger than him; they've been in the class together for four months. You almost deprived him of the chance to do his best. Most of the children that come here are from single-parent families. Little boys without a father are always looking for acceptance in other men's eyes. By you sitting him down at the wrong time, you would have taken away his chance to be accepted."

Chemah understood and bowed to Grandmaster in acknowledgment of his wisdom. Chemah saw the curly-haired boy standing alone attempting to take off his white belt. Chemah knew how difficult it could be for a grown-up to take off a sweat-soaked belt, much less for someone under seven. He walked over. "Let me help you with that, little man," he said, bending on one knee to help the little boy take his belt off. "How old are you?" Chemah asked as he got one knot loose on the belt.

"I'm five years old," the boy said seriously.

"Five years old?" Chemah said mocking surprise. "You sure are a big boy for five." This brought a big smile to the boy's face. "There you go," he said, loosening the last knot on the belt.

"Thank you," the boy whispered.

Chemah was touched by the boy's manners and soft demeanor after having witnessed him fight so ferociously. "My name is Sensei Chemah." He extended his hand in an offering of friendship. The boy shook his hand and smiled but did not speak. You know if you practice really hard, someday you can be a great fighter. The boy's smile widened but he didn't say anything else.

"What's your name, little man?" Chemah asked, tapping him on the chest in a playful manner.

"Tatsuya!" The curly-haired boy enunciated clearly as if he did not want to repeat it a second time.

"Tatsuya!" Chemah repeated. "That sounds like a strong name. Do you know what it means?"

Tatsuya shrugged his shoulders upward, admitting that he did not know.

"It means to have the characteristics of the Dragon," answered a female voice from behind Chemah. He turned to look over his shoulder and up into the eyes of Nairobi Kimble.

"Nairobi!" Chemah nearly shouted getting quickly to his feet.

"How are you, Chemah?" Nairobi asked coyly. She couldn't help herself; she still had feelings for him.

"What are you doing here?" Chemah asked, still in shock.

"Well, it's nice to see you, too," Nairobi said sarcastically.

"I'm sorry. I didn't mean to be rude. I'm just surprised to see you after all these years. How many years has it been? Six? Seven?" Chemah tried to answer his own question.

"Going on six years," Nairobi said, smiling.

"So what brings you here?" Chemah asked, trying to be nonchalant.

"I'm here to pick up my son," Nairobi said, holding her hand out for Tatsuya to take. "Tatsuya is your little boy?" Chemah asked with surprise.

"Our little boy," Nairobi corrected him as she stared into his face waiting for her words to sink in.

Chemah looked from Tatsuya back to Nairobi trying to make sense of what Nairobi had just said. "Ours—you mean like yours and mine," Chemah said, sounding stupid.

"Yes, yours and mine," Nairobi confirmed.

"How?" Chemah said loudly, sounding even more ridiculous. The parents and students who were still in the dojo were starting to stare at him.

"I don't think this is the place to have this discussion," Nairobi said, nodding toward Tatsuya, hoping that Chemah got her meaning. Chemah followed her eyes.

"Oh, you're right," Chemah conceded. "Is there a place we can talk?"

"Do you remember where my apartment is?" Nairobi responded. Chemah nodded yes. "Come by around ten tonight. Tatsuya should be asleep by then. We'll talk, okay?"

"Okay," Chemah said, still feeling a bit confused.

Tatsuya tugged on Chemah's hand and Chemah bent down to look at him squarely in the face. "Are you my daddy?" Tatsuya asked, sharing the gleam in Chemah's eyes.

"I think I am, Tatsuya," Chemah said, glancing up at Nairobi for a second.

"I heard the big boys talking," Tatsuya said in a hushed whisper. "They were pointing at you. They said you're 'The Dragon.'"

"Some people call me that," Chemah whispered, sharing Tatsuya's conspiratorial tone.

"Does that mean that I'm like you?" Tatsuya asked, wide-eyed.

"It means exactly that," Chemah said, beaming.

"I love you," Tatsuya said, grabbing Chemah around the neck and hugging him tightly.

Chemah was surprised not knowing what to do. He looked to Nairobi for assistance, but Nairobi was no help. She was too busy trying to wipe the tears out of her eyes. Chemah lifted Tatsuya up with the boy still clinging to his neck.

Chemah motioned to Nairobi. "Come on, I'll walk you guys outside to get a cab." Nairobi followed behind Chemah and Tatsuya in silence.

Chapter 12
What Will Be Was, But Will Be Again

Nairobi greeted Chemah at the door wearing what appeared to be the same sweat pants and T-shirt that she had worn the last time he was in her apartment six years ago. Chemah couldn't help notice that having a child had not changed Nairobi's body one bit, not to mention that her face still held the same natural beauty. The way she lingered in the doorway brought back a memory to Chemah that he always fondly recalled when things had gotten bad between him and Margarita.

"Hi," Nairobi said somewhat awkwardly.

"Hi."

"Come on in." She waved Chemah inside. "Tatsuya just went to sleep. I think he was trying to wait up for you. He knew you were coming over," she said, leading Chemah into the living room. Chemah noticed that the only thing in the room that had changed was the sofa.

"New sofa?" Chemah asked, making polite conversation as he sat down.

"Yeah, Tatsuya spilled a few glasses of juice on the last one; it was starting to look a bit grungy, so I got a new one." Nairobi sat down next to Chemah on the sofa. They looked at each other for what seemed like a full minute before Chemah broke the silence.

"Nairobi, why didn't you tell me I had a son?" Chemah asked.

Nairobi inhaled through her nose deeply before she began. "I didn't know I was pregnant until after you decided you weren't going to see me anymore. I wanted to tell you but I didn't want you to think I was trying to trap you."

Chemah licked his lips and swallowed trying to find some moisture in his mouth to aid him in speaking. "You could have told me." He found it difficult to speak knowing that Nairobi was right to believe he would have felt trapped.

"I did what I believed was best for me and my baby, Chemah," Nairobi said with the same gentleness that Chemah liked to remember.

"Well then, why tell me now?"

"Your son has been questioning me about who his father is for the past year. He's very smart, and I didn't know what to say to him anymore," she replied, throwing up her hands in dismay.

"How did you know I would go back to the dojo?" Chemah asked.

"I never knew you left. I wanted your son to see you at your best so I took him there. It was only after I didn't find you there that I realized it would be a good activity for Tatsuya to start. I never told him that we were going there to see his father," Nairobi explained.

"Do you mean to tell me that if I didn't show up at the dojo today I might never have known that I have a son?" Chemah asked.

"If I didn't find you at the dojo, I had every intention of depleting all of my resources to find you."

Chemah watched her, a frown crossing his face. "Then why didn't you?" he asked with a hint of sarcasm.

"I went to Grandmaster thinking that he might know how I could contact you. He took one look at Tatsuya and knew right away that he was your son. He said you looked exactly like Tatsuya when you were that age," Nairobi explained.

"Even Grandmaster Sam knew I had a son before I did," Chemah said, talking to himself.

"Grandmaster Sam suggested that I wait a while before trying to contact you. He seemed to know that you were coming back to the dojo soon."

Chemah had to smile at this information. When he was younger, Chemah would swear that Grandmaster Sam had ESP. Grandmaster always had information that no one else had. And seemed to know when things were going to happen. "So now that you found me, what do you expect to happen?" He knew immediately that it was a stupid thing to ask.

Nairobi's eyes narrowed as she glowered at Chemah. There was an unsettling silence before she spoke. "I don't need one fucking thing from you, Chemah," Nairobi spat. "And if that's all you have to say, you can get the fuck out of my home right now," she said as she stood.

Chemah jumped to his feet a split second after Nairobi and snatched her hand into his own. "I'm sorry. That was an ignorant thing to say." Chemah looked into her eyes for forgiveness.

"We can get a paternity test if you want." Nairobi said, still angry.

"I don't need a paternity test," Chemah said, still holding onto Nairobi's hand. "Stevie Wonder could see that he's my son," he added, trying to abate Nairobi's anger.

Nairobi smiled, then chuckled. "That was corny," she said, sitting back down.

Chemah sat down next to her, refusing to let go of her hand. "What do you want me to say?"

"The question shouldn't be, what do I want you to say. The question should be what, if anything, do you want to happen?" she dictated.

"I want to get to know my son."

"Then get to know your son, Chemah." Nairobi shot back. "That's why I brought him to you. He wants to get to know you, too, so what's the problem?"

Chemah hesitated for a moment, then spoke. "The problem is I'm married," he said, looking away from Nairobi.

Nairobi had not seen this coming. She never thought that Chemah could be married by now. "Married." She was stunned.

Chemah looked up from the floor. He saw the anger and hurt in Nairobi's eyes.

"For how long," she said flatly.

"Five years."

"So what are you trying to tell me?" she said with tears welling up in her eyes. "That because you have a wife and kids you don't have room to love another little boy?" Nairobi asked.

"No, no that's not it at all. I don't have any children," Chemah said, holding her hand tighter. "I mean, my wife and I never had any children," he corrected himself.

Nairobi wiped at the single tear that escaped her eyes. "No children? Why not? Why? Doesn't your wife want children?"

Chemah stared blankly at the floor again, ashamed of himself for being ashamed of his wife. "She can't have children," he said reluctantly.

"I'm sorry, Chemah. I didn't know. I just assumed—" Chemah waved away her embarrassment.

"It doesn't matter." Chemah looked up. "I'm happy that I have a son now. I'm just wondering how my wife is going to handle the news."

"Why? Doesn't she like children?"

"I think she'd love children if they were her own. Margarita has never brought the subject of children up again since the day we came from the fertility clinic."

"Your wife's name is Margarita?"

"Yes," Chemah said, nodding plainly.

"And you went to a fertility clinic to try and get pregnant?" Chemah nodded again.

Nairobi looked flustered. "I didn't even know you were married. I don't know why it never occurred to me that you could be married. I guess I didn't want to believe that you picked another woman over me."

Chemah look ashamed again. He opened his mouth to deny what Nairobi was saying, but nothing came out.

Nairobi quickly changed the subject. "Well, all that matters to me right now is that Tatsuya has a father who loves him and wants to spend time with him. Are you willing to do that, Chemah?"

"Of course," hr answered stiffly and sat up straight.

Nairobi and Chemah spent the next thirty minutes figuring out when would be the most suitable times for him to pick Tatsuya up and spend time with him. Chemah knew he should be discussing all of this with Margarita first, but he felt he had lost enough time with his son already and he was now prepared to take on all of his parental responsibilities. He'd just have to explain all of this to her when he got home. As Chemah and Nairobi were tying up their schedule plans, the intercom buzzer sounded. Nairobi left the couch to answer it.

"Yes?" Nairobi asked, pressing the talk button.

"John is here," the doorman spoke.

"Let him up, please," Nairobi answered.

"Yes, ma'am," the doorman responded and hung up his receiver.

"You're expecting company?" Chemah asked.

"I wasn't expecting anyone, but apparently my boyfriend can smell when another man is within ten feet of me."

Chemah had a sick feeling in his gut. "You have a boyfriend?" Chemah asked, trying to sound casual.

"Well, I call him a boyfriend, for lack of a better word," Nairobi answered. "John and I have been seeing each other on and off for the past two years. We've broken up and gotten back together so many times, sometimes I forget that we're even a couple."

"Maybe I should leave." Chemah got up to go.

"You don't have to go," Nairobi said half-heartedly. The doorbell rang and Nairobi's face seemed strained to remain relaxed. Chemah remained standing as he waited for Nairobi to open the door. Chemah heard Nairobi greet her boyfriend down the hall and explain that she had company. The male voice he heard talking to Nairobi was raised with contempt as she tried to explain to him who Chemah was, and why he was there. Chemah felt a wave of anger when he heard John push past Nairobi and rush down the hall to confront whomever this person was invading his territory.

Chemah was facing the living room entrance casually holding his hands in front of him. If John had known anything about body language, he would have deciphered that Chemah wasn't trying to hide anything. John had one foot inside the entrance to the living room when he started to raise his voice again.

"Who the fu—" John stopped himself as he stood completely inside the doorway to the living room. He had obviously expected to see someone unlike Chemah standing there.

Now confronted with the likes of Chemah, his tone changed. "Who are you?" John asked, nodding toward Chemah.

Chemah extended his right hand. "Hi, I'm Chemah, Tatsuya's father."

"You're what?" John asked, not bothering to shake Chemah's hand.

"I said I'm Tatsuya's father."

John was ignoring Chemah as he turned to face Nairobi, who had walked up behind him. "You never told me Tatsuya's father was a nigger."

"What the fuck did you say?" Chemah grabbed John by the throat with one hand and pinned him against the wall before he could utter another word. John was desperately using both hands to get Chemah to release him, as he felt he would be losing consciousness soon. Chemah's eyes were ablaze with loathing as he stared into the scared eyes of this pig. Then he turned his hate onto Nairobi. "Is this the kind of pathetic shit you've been subjecting my son to, huh, is it?"

"Let him go, Chemah; you're killing him. Look at what you're doing. Let him go!" Nairobi screamed.

Chemah let John loose right before he sensed he would lose consciousness. John fell to the floor gasping and clutching his own neck as if he thought Chemah's fingers were still attached. "You could have killed me," he said, glaring up at Chemah.

"You remember that shit for the next time you decide to call someone a nigger," Chemah said, glaring right back at him. "I'm leaving, Nairobi," he announced. "Do you want me to take this piece of shit out with me?" he asked, pointing to the broken man on the floor.

"I'll take care of it, Chemah," Nairobi said.

Not knowing what else to do, Chemah headed for the door. "I'll call you tomorrow," he called back to Nairobi who was busy trying to help John up. Chemah looked over his shoulder to see John pushing Nairobi's helping hand away from him. Chemah shook his head in disgust. *Why do all the good women end up with all of the assholes?* he thought.

Chemah pressed the down button to call for the elevator and the answer to his own question hit him like a slap to his face. *Because all the so-called good men wouldn't know a good woman if they tripped over one.*

The elevator came, and Chemah got in and pressed the "G" button. As the elevator went down, so went Chemah's spirit. He couldn't shake the feeling that he was leaving something terribly important behind. Chemah walked out of the building suppressing the urge to go back upstairs and claim Nairobi as his own. That urge was only tempered by the anxiety he felt about how Margarita would react when he explained to her that he has a son. And that he already loved him very much.

Chapter 13
KNOW HIM, KNOW YOU, NO ME

Chemah had picked Tatsuya up fifteen minutes earlier. He was driving Margarita's new Jaguar. It was triple white from the convertible top to the leather steering wheel. His old Beemer had finally croaked two weeks ago and he hadn't yet decided what he was going to replace it with. He had been on the phone ordering a cab to take him downtown, when Margarita snatched the phone from his hand and pressed the off button. "What …"

Normally Margarita wouldn't allow anyone to drive her car, but she was full of surprises these days. "What the hell do you think you're doing?" Margarita asked.

"I'm ordering a cab so that I can go pick up Tatsuya," Chemah answered, holding back his anger. He and Margarita had been arguing on and off since the day he had come home and told her about Tatsuya and Nairobi. She had insisted that he get a DNA test, and he had flatly refused, saying, "I know he's mine."

They had come to a compromise of sorts as Margarita realized she was not going to win this argument. Margarita announced that she was going to have a background check done on Nairobi to see what she had been up to for the past five years or so.

"You can do whatever the fuck you want to do," he snarled at her in the heat of the argument. "You just leave my son out of it." Chemah had never used this tone with her before, and she was taken aback, but it had not taken any of the steam out of her. She would do whatever she needed to keep another woman away from her man. Now, here she was about to start another round of arguing right before he was going to pick his son up.

"I thought we had agreed that your son would be an addition to our family, on the days that you have custody of him," Margarita said sarcastically.

"That's right, that's what I said." Chemah held back, not wanting to waste time with another fight.

"Well, that does mean that he'll be my son, too, doesn't it?" Margarita continued.

"Yes, that's what it means," Chemah said patiently.

"Then let me ask you one last question, if you don't mind," Margarita mocked.

"Go ahead," Chemah said dryly.

"Do you think I would let any son of mine come home in a shitty beat-up Town Car, driven by some illegal alien African who probably doesn't even have a license?"

Chemah waited not knowing what to say. Margarita reached for his left hand. Chemah almost pulled it away. Margarita brought his rough hand to her lip-gloss moistened lips, and kissed his knuckles gently in a theatrical display of submission. When she released his hand, Chemah felt the weight of her keys in his palm. "Bring our son home in style," she said, sounding a bit siddity.

Chemah was happy with Margarita's sudden change in attitude. He hadn't bothered to say anything else. He'd just accepted the keys as a peace offering and anxiously left to get his son.

Chemah pulled up to the brownstone that he and Margarita had lived in for the past five years, and realized that there had never been a child in the house. He tried to recall if any visiting friends had brought over their children and still came up with a zero. Shit, not even one who came for a visit.

"Are we there yet?" Tatsuya asked, taking him out of his reverie.

"Yep, this is it," Chemah announced. Tatsuya undid his own seatbelt, and Chemah was out of the car to open his door before the boy could jump into the busy street. Chemah took Tatsuya's hand into his own; it felt warm and comfortable. They walked hand in hand toward the brownstone and were both startled when the door appeared to be opening of its own volition as they approached. Margarita came from behind the door before Chemah could get Tatsuya to move forward again. Margarita planned for her introduction to take place at the threshold of her domain. Before Margarita could extend a greeting to Tatsuya, the little boy had retreated behind his father's leg.

Margarita fixed her face in an exaggerated pout and bent down so that she might be at eye level with the little boy. "Did I scare you?" she spoke softly to the little boy. Tatsuya poked his head out from behind his father's leg, and shook his head no. "Oh of course you're not afraid of me." She took another strategy. "Did your father tell you all about me?"

Tatsuya came entirely from behind his father's leg. "You're my stepmother," he said, looking down at the floor.

"Well, I bet no one told you how great it is to have a stepmother, did they?" Tatsuya shook his head no. "Well then you'll be very surprised to find that you and I are going to be the closest of friends. Now take my hand and I'll show you around the house and to your very own new room." Tatsuya looked up at his father for approval, and when Chemah nodded his head giving Tatsuya the go-ahead, the little boy reluctantly took Margarita's hand and allowed himself to be led into the house. Margarita looked over her shoulder at Chemah, winked at him, and blew him a kiss as she led Tatsuya.

"This is the living room," she said, waving her hand across the air in such an exaggerated way that she looked like a Black Vanna White exposing a prize that he had just won.

"Is my room under the stairs?" Tatsuya asked, looking up at Margarita with an expression that said he was unmoved by her enthusiasm with her own living room.

She looked down at Tatsuya in mock horror, then looked at Chemah in a plea for help. Chemah folded his arms and raised an eyebrow in answer to Margarita's plea. He was getting a kick out of seeing her struggle with winning over Tatsuya. Chemah had seen Margarita charm herself into and out of many things with ease, but never did he see her as ill at ease as she was now. Margarita and Tatsuya were both looking at each other as if waiting for answers.

Chemah was about to intercede when Margarita broke the silence. She took Tatsuya's hand. "Come sit over here with me for a second," she said, leading him to her red couch. Margarita sat down first, then patted the space next to her indicating to Tatsuya that he should sit there. Tatsuya obediently sat on the exact spot where Margarita had patted, as if he did not want to do any less or more than what she said. "Who told you that you would have a room under the stairs?" she asked, using a hurt voice Chemah had never heard her use.

"Nobody," Tatsuya answered, shrugging his shoulder.

"Then why would you ever think that we would ever give you a room under the stairs?" she asked.

"I saw it in a movie," Tatsuya answered, looking at the floor.

"What movie?"

"Harry Potter," Tatsuya mumbled.

Margarita had strained to hear him. "Harry who?" she asked carefully.

Tatsuya looked up from the floor right into her eyes. *"HARRY POTTER,"* Tatsuya answered clearly this time.

"What's a Hairy Potter?" she asked, looking quizzically at Tatsuya.

"Not Hairy Potter, *Harry Potter,"* Tatsuya corrected her.

"Okay, *Harry Potter,"* Margarita responded. "Who is he?"

Tatsuya took a deep breath as if exasperated by her question, then launched into telling the story of a magical little boy who lived under the stairs of the family home where he had been left. Tatsuya told the story with all the zeal and imagination of a five-year-old boy, and Margarita listened intently, ooohing and showing shock and surprise as if on cue every time Tatsuya's voice lowered or raised for effect. When Tatsuya finished his story he was almost out of breath from the speed and enthusiasm of which he told it. Margarita took the moment that he paused to catch his breath as her cue to talk.

"Well, that was a wonderful story, Tatsuya," she said, taking his hand in hers, "and I can see why you'd be concerned about having a room under the stairs, but I promise you that as long as I live you'll never ever have to live under anyone's stairs." Tatsuya smiled up at Margarita, seeming to make up in his mind that it was now all right to like her. "Now, before we go upstairs to see your room, why don't we go into the kitchen and have a big bowl of ice cream?" Tatsuya nodded with enthusiasm. Tatsuya and Margarita popped up off the couch at the same time as if they shared one mind. She took his hand again and started to lead him toward the kitchen. She was almost at the door to the kitchen before she looked over her shoulder to address Chemah.

"Honey, don't you want some ice cream, too?" Tatsuya had also turned around and his hand was extended out for Chemah to take.

Chemah was glad that Margarita had won over Tatsuya. He'd had visions of Tatsuya hating his new stepmother, thereby making him her enemy. Chemah liked the feeling of having a complete family now, even if it would only be on the weekends. "Just ice cream? How about some cake, too?" he said as he walked across the room.

"YEAH," Tatsuya cheered. Margarita pursed her lips at Chemah letting him know that she didn't appreciate him stealing any part of her new popularity with Tatsuya. Chemah smirked as he took Tatsuya's free hand and led them both into the kitchen. "And maybe we can find some sprinkles to go with the cake and ice cream."

"YEAH," Tatsuya wailed.

"And some nuts."

"YEAH."

"And some whipped cream."

"YEAH."

"And a stomachache," Margarita interjected before they could go any further.

Chemah and Tatsuya both stopped dead in their tracks. Tatsuya looked up at Margarita with a graveness that was uncommon for someone his age. "That's not funny," he said, shaking his head.

For a second Margarita thought she had lost him. Instinctively she bent down and kissed him on the forehead. "Don't worry, I'll always know how to make it better." Those words brought the smile back on Tatsuya's face.

Damn, Chemah thought, *she used that same line on me five years ago.*

Chapter 14
FUNNY AIN'T THE WORD FOR IT

Nairobi was waiting in front of her open apartment door for the elevator to open. This was the first time her son had slept away from her since he was born, and she was anxious to see him again. When the doorman announced that Tatsuya and Chemah were on their way up, Nairobi had rushed to the door to greet them without considering her appearance. Nairobi now saw her reflection in the elevator window and wished she had taken the time to comb her hair. Feeling self-conscious as she looked at herself, she began to comb her fingers through her hair in an attempt to undo the damage that the sweat of her aerobic workout had inflicted.

Chemah and Tatsuya came bursting through the elevator door still laughing from a joke they had shared on the way up to the apartment. They were both surprised to see Nairobi waiting for them and simultaneously covered their mouths to stifle the laughter that was spilling from them. They both straightened up attempting their best to appear serious.

"Hello, Nairobi." Chemah smiled.

"Hello, Mommy," Tatsuya chimed in. Like twins that could anticipate each other's thoughts, the father and son looked at each other again and busted out laughing uncontrollably.

Nairobi folded her arms and eyed the father and son suspiciously. She believed that somehow they were having a good laugh at her expense. "And what may I ask is so funny?" Chemah became serious immediately, but Tatsuya continued to giggle behind his hands.

Chemah scooped Tatsuya up into his arms and gave him a great big hug and kiss. "I need to speak to your mother for a little while," Chemah said to him. "Why don't you go inside and wash up? Remember, I'll be seeing you at the karate school on Thursday, so practice those kicks we talked about."

"Okay, Daddy," Tatsuya said, giving Chemah a quick hug. Chemah put Tatsuya down, and he ran at his apartment door at full speed. He looked like an imitation of a Roadrunner cartoon as he stopped instantly one inch from smacking his face against the hard cold surface of the iron door. Tatsuya turned the knob and then turned to wave to his father before going inside. Chemah waved back, and Tatsuya slowly closed the door, seeming reluctant to say goodbye. When the door finally closed, Chemah turned his attention back to Nairobi. Nairobi still had her arms folded in front of her, and didn't appear to be happy.

"And what was that all about?" Nairobi asked before Chemah could say anything else.

"What?" Chemah said, surprised by Nairobi's tone.

"Whaaat?" Nairobi mocked him. "You know what, all the secrecy, and the laughing," she said, looking hurt.

"Oh that," Chemah said sheepishly. "We were just telling each other jokes," he confessed.

"Telling each other jokes?" Nairobi said, obviously not believing a word from Chemah.

"Yeah, you know, why did the chicken cross the road and all that kind of stuff."

"Why did the chicken cross the road is not that funny," Nairobi said, still not believing him.

"Well, I kind of ran out of those kind of jokes, so I told him one that was a little more mature."

"More mature?" Nairobi asked, now tapping her foot.

"Well, kind of," Chemah responded, now looking guilty. "I sort of told him he shouldn't tell anyone else the joke. That's why he was trying to stop laughing," Chemah attempted to explain.

"I leave you with my son for one weekend, and already you have him trying to keep secrets from me," Nairobi accused, still not trying to hear Chemah's explanation.

"No, it's not like that," Chemah tried to explain again.

"Tell me the joke!" Nairobi demanded.

"It's a kid joke; it's really not that funny," Chemah said offhandedly.

"I said, I want to hear the joke," Nairobi said through clenched teeth.

"Alright, alright," Chemah relented, "but I'm telling you it's not that funny."

"I'll be the judge of that."

"Okay," Chemah started, "there were two cannibals eating a clown. One cannibal says to the other, does this taste funny to you?"

Nairobi watched Chemah, waiting for him to say something else. "That's it, that's what all the secret was about?"

"What did you expect? A tits and ass joke? The kid's only five years old."

Nairobi was finding it hard to apologize. "I don't know what I was expecting," she finally admitted. "I guess I was a little worried about leaving him with anyone else. It's been just him and me for so long, and there are just so many bad things happening in this city, I don't think I've slept since you two left on Friday," Nairobi admitted.

"Listen, everything was cool this weekend. Tatsuya got to know me better, I got to know him better, and he and Margarita are becoming pretty good friends." Chemah's last sentence had hurt Nairobi, but she'd be damned if she let Chemah know it.

"I'm glad he's getting along with your wife," she lied. "Listen, why don't you come in for a second, and sit down. I'll make some coffee and I have some delicious Junior's cheesecake that my friend brings me whenever she goes to Brooklyn."

Chemah looked thoughtful for a second. "I'd love to," he said, "but I really don't want any trouble with your boyfriend."

"Good, then you can come in. I got rid of him the last time you saw him. I told him I couldn't be with anyone that used the word 'nigger' the way that he did."

"Hey, you just used the word 'nigger,'" Chemah joked.

"Yeah, but that's 'cause I'm down," Nairobi said, folding her arms against her chest and leaning back, mocking a New York thug. Chemah laughed.

"Who's teaching you ebonics now?" he asked, grabbing her around the waist and leading her into the apartment.

"No one is teaching me. I watch MTV." Nairobi laughed.

"May I suggest for our son's sake that you stop trying to be down," Chemah said, closing the door behind him.

"And why should I?" Nairobi asked, continuing the conversation as she walked up the hall toward the living room. "Don't you think at least one of his parents should be cool?"

"He already has one cool parent," Chemah said, following close behind her.

"Yeah, you're so cool, I think I'll call you Coolo," Nairobi said, laughing.

"You think that's real funny, don't you?" Chemah said, mushing the back of her head. He knew Coolo meant asshole in New York\Puerto Rican slang.

Chapter 15
AND I JUST LOOKED AROUND AND SHE'S GONE

It was seven o'clock p.m. when Margarita attempted to call Chemah at work. A police officer had called from the Eighty-First Precinct explaining to her that Tatsuya had this phone number at his school to be contacted in case of an emergency. From the outset, the officer had asked to speak to Chemah Rivers. Initially, Margarita had assumed it was an officer from his own precinct. She wondered if he wasn't at work, where he could be. When the officer explained that they were holding Tatsuya and trying to contact a parent or guardian to pick him up, Margarita immediately asked what the problem was. The police officer refused to talk about it over the phone and asked if she had a way of contacting Mr. Rivers. Margarita explained to the officer that her husband was a police detective at the Eighty-First Precinct.

"Jesus, I should've known," the officer said. "How many Chemah Rivers could there be in the city? I'm sorry to have bothered you at home, ma'am. I'll call down to his precinct right away."

Margarita knew that Chemah enjoyed some notoriety within the fraternal order of cops. He was the only detective with dreads on the high-profile crimes team.

"What precinct is the child at right now?" Margarita asked. "I'll come down to pick him up, and meet my husband there."

"Thank you, Mrs. Rivers." The officer was being friendlier now. "We're at the Forty-Fourth. When you get here, ask for Officer McCoy. Everyone knows me; I'm the Community Affairs Officer."

When Margarita hung up the phone, she dialed the number to Chemah's office trying to reach him before Officer McCoy. When she found out that he was in the field, she left a message for him to call her and ran upstairs to get a jacket. It was November now and she had heard on the radio that it was eighteen degrees. She went into her closet to get her fox, and changed her mind at the last minute knowing that her husband would not appreciate the stares she would receive at the precinct. After a few seconds of indecision she picked out a hooded, mink-lined DKNY jacket with a GoreTex shell exterior. No one would know she had fur on, and she could still be comfortable and warm. As she looked into the mirror, it dawned on her that Tatsuya was alone at the precinct and probably very scared.

"You self-absorbed bitch," she said to herself out loud. "You've got to start thinking like a mother," she said, talking to herself in whispers as she took the stairs two at a time. When she reached the door, she looked back at her living room to see if she had forgotten anything. "My bag," she said to herself as she spotted the handbag with her keys in it. The fact that the bag didn't match her jacket gnawed at her sensibilities, but she continued to walk out of the house and toward her car.

Margarita turned over the ignition of her car and felt the powerful Jaguar engine come to life. She usually liked to sit in the seat for a couple of moments and feel the power of the car before taking off, but today she felt the urgency of Tatsuya sitting alone at the police precinct overwhelming her. She put the car in reverse and turned around slowly, backing the car as close as she could to the car behind her. She was mindful to keep a safe enough distance that there was no chance she would scratch the paint. Margarita put the car into drive and turned her head to the left to make sure that no other cars were coming in her direction. She then allowed her foot to gradually come off the brake and turned the steering wheel left, allowing the car to glide into the street on its own idling power.

When Margarita knew she was clear of the parked cars that had kept her boxed in, she came to life behind the wheel. She shifted her car into overdrive and pressed sharply on the gas pedal. The power she felt behind the wheel of a Jaguar was akin to controlling a man that didn't want to be controlled. She smiled to herself as she sped down Sugar Hill narrowly missing a man in a leather jacket crossing the street against the light. She looked in the rearview mirror in time to see him mouth *fucking bitch*. She couldn't hold back the giggles as she saw him look behind himself to check for more cars coming. "That'll learn 'em," she said, imitating a Southern drawl.

She turned her full attention back to the road, but the thought of Tatsuya alone crept back into her mind. She felt a fierce anger at the thought of him fending off strangers at the police station. She grit her teeth and gave the car more power, aware that she was doing sixty miles per hour in a thirty miles-per-hour zone. Margarita's maternal instincts were taking over and the feelings gave her life a sense of purpose again. "There better not be anybody fucking with my boy in that place," she said out loud in a voice so gruff she hardly recognized it as her own.

She looked up through her windshield and saw clouds start to develop. She thought of the adage her grandmother was fond of reciting. *'Clouds bring the rain, and rain sings the song of cleansing. We need a good rain.'* It took her another ten minutes to get across town and when she pulled in front of the precinct she ignored all of the parking signs, pulling into a spot designated for police vehicles. When Chemah's BMW was no longer running, she had relieved him of his police placard. She took it out of the glove compartment and placed it in the window.

She walked away from the car quickly and she ran up the stairs in front of the building surprising herself as she took two at a time. Before walking through the precinct doors, she made an imperceptible gesture with her hand, pressing the button that activated her car alarm. The alarm sound reassured her that the Jag was safe. The fact that it was sitting in front of a police precinct did not mean that her car would be safe.

This precinct was located in a part of the Upper West Side that wasn't totally gentrified yet. There were still some Latinos in the area and as much as Margarita loved her Latino people, word had it that car theft was still a large source of income for them, even this close to the police station. She was proud of her heritage, but shit, this was a Jag.

The minute Margarita saw the sargeant at the front desk, she knew he was going to be useless to her. Margarita walked right to the desk, which looked more like a kitchen counter than a desk, and attempted to get the sargeant's attention by rapping the flat of her hand against its top twice. The sargeant was in the midst of filling out a log of some sort, but looked up before Margarita's hand fell on the desk the second time.

"I'll be with you in a moment, Miss. Just sit over there and wait a second," he said, waving toward the bench as if to dismiss her. Margarita didn't budge. The sargeant looked up again, and took a deep breath as if he were gathering his patience.

"I'm here to find out about my son—" Margarita started.

The sargeant cut her off. "Miss, if you'll just wait a minute, I'll—"

"Is Captain Forrest still in charge here?" Margarita spoke over him this time.

"What's that?" the sargeant asked.

"I said, get Captain Forrest on the phone and tell him that Margarita Smith Rivers is in his precinct."

The sargeant was not used to being spoken to in this manner and didn't respond immediately to Margarita. The two stared at each other for moments before the sargeant decided that it was better to be safe than sorry. He picked up the phone and punched four numbers on the phone pad before turning his back to Margarita, whom in turn pretended she wasn't trying to listen to his conversation. Soon the sargeant was off the phone and turned back to Margarita. "The captain will be right down to see you, Mrs. Rivers. If there's anything I can get you while you're waiting, please let me know."

Margarita pretended she didn't hear him, and leaned in closer to hear him repeat his words. The sargeant leaned closer into his desk and gritted his teeth for a second before saying in a low and respectable tone, "If there's anything I can get you while you're waiting, please don't hesitate to ask."

"Nothing, thank you, Sargeant." She turned toward Captain Forrest who was descending the stairs.

Captain Forrest and Margarita had known each other for three years. During the current mayor's election campaign, Captain Forrest had volunteered his services, and was assigned to work with Margarita. She found that the captain was an effective leader. Initially she had given him easy assignments, but after having proved himself time and again, she had brought him into the inner workings of the campaign. Later, they had gained a mutual respect for one another as they realized a mutual need for power and control.

When the captain reached the bottom of the stairs, the sargeant immediately realized that he had underestimated the woman in front of him. The sargeant had never seen the captain defer to anyone the way he was doing with this woman.

Captain Forrest reached the bottom of the stairs and held out both hands to embrace Margarita. "It's nice to see you, Margarita," he said, giving her a gentle squeeze. "I'm sorry that the only time you've had to come and visit is during this time of tragedy."

"You know why I'm here?" she asked.

"I'm afraid so. One of the detectives on the case informed me that he talked to you a while ago."

"I thought it was the Community Affairs Officer I spoke to."

"Yes it was, but that just means he's on desk duty until he recuperates from his injuries."

"Oh, I see," Margarita remarked, not really caring about the politics of the precinct.

"Until that detective talked to you, no one realized that we had Chemah's son in our custody. Hell, we didn't even know Chemah had a son," the captain admitted.

"Is he alright? Where is he?" she asked, careful to keep her excitement under control.

"He's with the Community Affairs Officer and a Children's Services worker that we had to call in."

"Children's Services worker? Why did you have to call a children's services worker?"

"Calm down, Margarita," the captain said, pulling her away from the desk sargeant's hearing range. "This is standard procedure when a parent doesn't pick a child up from school."

"I don't understand. Have you found out why his mother didn't pick him up?"

Captain Forrest was at odds with his own behavior for a second. It was unlike him to break protocol, but he thought it would be all right given that it was

Margarita. Captain Forrest took Margarita gently by the elbow again and led her further away from listening ears. When the captain stopped, he looked around to see who was nearby. It was obvious that the sargeant was attempting to look busy in front of his commanding officer. All of the other officers around were either coming or going and seemed to pay them no attention.

"Maybe we should talk about this in my office," the captain began.

"You know me, Dennis. If it's something important, tell me right here, and right now."

The captain looked around again before looking Margarita in the eyes. "The boy's mother was found dead in her apartment," he said quietly.

Margarita's eyes went wide with horror. She covered her mouth with one hand and sucked in a breath so hard that it made her gasp for a second breath immediately.

The captain caught Margarita by the shoulders. "Are you alright?" he asked, concerned that telling her had been a mistake.

Margarita held up her right hand and nodded that she was okay as she attempted to catch her breath. "I'm alright. I just need a second," she said, still fending the captain off with her hand as she attempted to compose herself. After a second she stood upright and appeared in control of the world again. She looked steadily at the captain and he recognized the look of determination she wore when she was about to give direction. The captain knew the look well, but didn't appreciate it in his domain.

"Was Chemah already told?"

"No, not yet. When I found out it was his son, I called his captain immediately and told him what was going on. His captain would have only told him that we have his son in our custody. He's being driven here as we speak."

"Good, now show me where my son is, Captain Forrest."

The captain didn't like being ordered, and decided that it was time to wrest control from Margarita before she got out of hand. "I think we'd better go to my office and wait for Chemah to come before you see the boy," he suggested.

Margarita changed her tactic. "Dennis, I want to see him now. He must be scared to death in this place, not knowing a single person."

The captain set his jaw and spoke with a measure of authority. "You're not his legal guardian and you cannot see him without your husband being present, Margarita." Margarita started to object, but knew better than to question this man's authority in public. The captain's voice softened when he saw that she'd acquiesced. "We'll wait for Chemah in my office. I'll have the sargeant escort him directly there when he walks through the door."

Margarita nodded in agreement. Captain Forrest walked back to the sargeant and gave him instructions before returning to Margarita and escorting her up the stairs. Halfway, Margarita turned around and addressed the desk sargeant. "Sargeant, would you be a dear and get us a cup of coffee?" The sargeant's eyes darted to his captain's, almost pleading for him not to approve. In return the captain gave him an almost imperceptible nod, okaying the sargeant to do as she requested.

"Yes, Ma'am," he answered. "How would you like that?"

"Black and sweet," she said, locking eyes with him for a second before turning to follow the captain up the stairs.

The captain sat behind his desk and looked up at Margarita, whose eyes were attempting to bore into his. "Margarita, it's best this way," he said, trying to sound convincing.

"My only concern is for Tatsuya. The boy must be frightened out of his mind."

"Tat who?" Margarita's face was an ice grill. "Oh, you mean the boy." Captain Forrest smiled, trying to ignore the look on her face. "That little boy of yours couldn't be in better hands," he said, acknowledging her claim of motherhood. The captain could tell that his words were having their desired effect. "You know when the boys found out whose kid we had here, they started tripping over themselves trying to make sure he was okay. I'm told almost every cop in the building has looked in on him at least once."

Margarita looked at him puzzled. "Why would everyone go through all that trouble?"

"Didn't you know your husband is a legend in the department?" the captain asked, looking at Margarita as if she were the one pulling his leg.

She looked wryly at him. "I know Chemah has helped to solve quite a few high-profile crimes, but I doubt if that would qualify him as a legend," Margarita answered.

"Are you trying to tell me that Chemah has never told you about what happened to him after his first couple of months in the academy?" Margarita pursed her lips in an exaggerated manner and shook her head no. "Well, I should have known he wouldn't have ever mentioned it to you. That's just the type of guy he is; never bigs himself up. I don't think you were married at the time, were you?" Margarita shook her head no.

Captain Dennis Forrest was too pleased with himself. Here was a woman who prided herself on knowing everything about everyone that was worth knowing. Although he considered her an ally and colleague, he was happy to have information she was not privy to.

Sitting up straight in his chair the captain felt like a conspirator about to divulge top-secret information. "I've only heard this story secondhand, but I've heard it told the same way at least ten different times. The story goes like this. There was a fellow cadet having some trouble learning some of the self-defense techniques that they were teaching in the academy, so Chemah decided to take the kid aside and help him with the techniques during their lunch hour. After a few days the kid has the techniques down like a pro. Pretty soon after that, anybody that's having trouble with the self-defense part of the academy training is coming to Chemah for pointers. Anyway, one of the academy self- defense trainers gets wind of how Chemah is helping out the other cadets and gets it in his mind that Chemah is trying to show up the academy trainers. So this instructor decides to teach Chemah a lesson.

"One day he calls Chemah onto the training floor in front of all the other cadets to 'demonstrate' how to take down a perp with the most recent technique that they taught," he continued. "Anyway, this guy has no idea of Chemah's skill level and just tells Chemah to attack him. So, Chemah attacks, but everyone can see it's halfhearted. The instructor tries once, tries twice, tries three times, and still can't take Chemah down. So now the other instructors are watching and even though they know this instructor is a real asshole, they also know they have to back him. This time Chemah has to demonstrate what he would do if he were surrounded and attacked by four attackers. According to the way other cops who were there described the way Chemah took those guys apart, it was a work of art."

Margarita sat with her arms crossed and felt a certain disdain at how Captain Forrest glorified her husband's exploits. She interrupted his story. "So Chemah beat up four police officers that were probably due to be put in their place anyway, and a bunch of testosterone-driven cadets makes him their hero." She was unimpressed.

Captain Forrest seemed amused by Margarita's interruption. "You have it all wrong, Margarita. Let me tell you the rest of the story. The next day Chemah was called into the office of the commanding officer of the academy. The C.O. had been told what had occurred by one of the instructors and apparently he thought that it would be a good idea to have Chemah under his command at the academy."

"The commanding officer of the police academy can ask for someone to be assigned to the academy, and it's done just like that?" Margarita interrupted again.

His smile broadened. "Margarita, we both know what a well-placed phone call by the right person can accomplish." She looked sheepish, but kept quiet as the he nodded knowingly. "As you're well aware, Chemah has never taught one day at the academy. That's because he turned the C.O. down flat."

Margarita hadn't known this bit of information, but wasn't surprised. She shook her head. "Just like him," she said under her breath.

"Working at the academy is one of the sweetest posts an officer can get, and you know what Chemah said to him. Chemah says, 'I want to do my time on the street like everyone else.' He tells him, 'I just want to learn the job like my fellow officers.'" He chuckled. "I still can't believe that shit. All of the cadets at the academy heard about it, and damn near threw him a party. So, now you can understand why all the officers here are climbing all over themselves to keep his kid comfortable. It might sound corny, but Chemah symbolizes to these guys all the reasons that they took this job in the first place."

The captain's phone rang, and he held a hand up signaling Margarita to wait a second while he took the call. He listened for a second, said "thank you" into the receiver, and then hung up. "Your husband is here," he said, getting up from his desk.

She got up almost simultaneously, as Chemah pushed in the door to the captain's office. Chemah took a moment to look around the room. "Where's Tatsuya?" he said to Margarita without bothering to acknowledge the captain. Margarita paused for a moment, then looked toward the captain, content that he would be the one who would have to explain.

Chemah took his cue from her and turned toward the captain. "Sir?" he said with an accusatory tone.

"Detective, please have a seat." The captain gestured to the empty seat next to Margarita. "I was just explaining to your wife that your son is perfectly safe, and you'll get to see him in a few minutes. I really don't want to detain you from seeing him any longer than I have to, but I think it's better that you hear this from me now, before the detectives ask you any questions."

Chemah sat at the edge of his chair looking back and forth from Margarita who was staring intensely at the floor to the captain whom Chemah's instinct told him was trying to size him up somehow.

The captain found his voice. "Chemah, your son's mother was found dead in her apartment earlier this evening."

Chemah didn't react immediately. He was concentrating on the captain's lips, waiting for them to form some other words that his mind could more easily grasp. The captain felt uneasy waiting for a response and began to squirm in his seat. The look on Chemah's face changed distinctly from disbelief to anger. He stood up slowly, biting his lip to distinguish reality from the ghost pain he felt in his chest.

Captain Forrest mirrored Chemah's movement getting up from his seat slowly. "I'm sorry for your loss, Chemah," he said, and immediately wished he hadn't said anything.

Chemah looked as if he were doing everything to control himself to keep from lunging at the captain and ripping him to shreds.

"Nairobi's dead?" Chemah couldn't believe it.

The captain just nodded this time, but Chemah just seemed to be looking through him anyway. Margarita stood up and reached out to embrace her husband. Without even looking at her, his hand came up quickly stopping an inch in front of her face. It had a whiplashing effect on her. Her head snapped back to avoid being struck.

"I'm alright," he said, focusing his attention back on Captain Forrest. "How did she die, sir?" Chemah asked, still hoping that somehow a mistake had been made.

"There was a blunt trauma to the head, but we're still unsure of how it occurred. She may have been hit with something. I have Phil Masserette on it. He's the expert in these situations."

Chemah nodded his approval. "Yeah, I know Phil. He's a good guy. Uh, do you think maybe I could go to the crime scene and lend a hand, Captain?" Chemah asked.

"I don't think that would be a good idea, Chemah. You're too close to this case. There could be a conflict of interest if we decide this is a homicide. Besides it's out of your jurisdiction, and I doubt if your captain is going to lend you out on something like this. Besides, Chemah, right now your son needs you more than we ever will. I couldn't allow your wife to see him without you, because she's not legally his guardian, and I didn't want anyone to say we weren't going by the book on this one."

"I can appreciate that, Captain. Thank you."

"Oh, you know I'm just covering my own ass on this," the captain admitted. "If there's anything I can do for you now, you just let me know."

"There's nothing I can think of right now, sir, except I'd like to take my son home now," he requested.

"Of course," the captain said, coming from behind his desk, and leading the way out of his office. As they walked down the hall, all eyes were on Chemah. News had spread that he was in the building, and those who knew what was going on came away from their desks to pay their respects. Other officers who were in different stages of getting dressed or undressed in the locker room had hurried just so they could pat him on the back or tip their hat in salute.

Walking directly behind Chemah, Margarita was in awe. When she had initially come into the building, the place had seemed almost empty. Now the whole place had come to life, and it was obvious that it was her husband's presence that had resuscitated it. For his part Chemah seemed to take everything in stride. He waved to officers that waved to him and shook hands with almost everyone who crossed his path. He seemed to know a lot of officers by name.

Captain Forrest came to a door that said "Detectives," grasped the door knob, twisted and pushed the door open wide without stepping over the threshold. On the other side of the door, Tatsuya was sitting on a swivel chair at a large oak desk. He was surrounded by five men. Each one had a detective shield exposed, and each had a slice of pizza in his hand and a smile on his face. Tatsuya himself had a mouth full of pizza and was in mid-bite when he saw his father on the other side of the door. His eyes went wide and drops of pizza juice dribbled onto his chin as his open-mouthed crooked smile was displayed.

The five detectives turned toward the door simultaneously to see what had drawn his attention. When they saw Chemah walking through the door, they all stood erect and became somber. Tatsuya jumped out of his chair and ran to his father. He didn't have long to run as his father's steps doubled at the sight of him. Chemah bent down and opened his arms letting the boy crash into his chest. Tatsuya hugged his father tightly around the neck and Chemah was reminded of the first time they had met.

The five men stood staring at the father and son for a moment each with a measure of sadness and grace in his eyes. "I've got some work to do," one of the men grumbled under his breath. That seemed to be the cue for breaking up their small gathering. Each man grumbled an excuse of his own and went about gathering belongings before swiftly exiting the room. Margarita walked into the detective's offices behind Chemah, aware that neither the young boy nor the father needed her at this time.

On the far side of the room a lone figure sat watching the interaction of the boy and his father. As Margarita came into Ms. Dooser's line of vision, the woman turned her eyes on Margarita who was being scanned from head to toe. The woman's eyes were digitizing information before storing it in her brain for a report to be written later at the Protective Services for Children's downtown office.

Ms. Dooser was renowned for her detailed reports at the office. It was her claim to fame and the one thing her anal-retentive personality allowed her to do without making people sick of her. Ms. Dooser loved her job. She always thought if only she didn't have to deal with some of these dreadful Negroes, her job would be perfect. It wasn't that she was racist or anything like that. She just preferred to deal with people who were more like her. After all her mother had taught her that those types of people could not help themselves. *'They were just born like that.'*

When she finished her clinical inspection of Margarita, she stood up and walked toward the woman with an extended hand. "Hi, my name is Ms. Dooser. I'm with Protective Services for Children."

Margarita extended her hand to the older woman and smiled cordially. "Nice to meet you, Ms. Dooser. I'm Mrs. Rivers, Tatsuya's stepmother."

The older woman didn't even try to conceal her surprise. "Oh, no one told me the boy had a stepmother. I went through his school record and it had no mention of a stepmother."

Margarita felt like punching this bitch in the mouth, but had not gotten where she was in life by losing her composure in awkward situations. "I'm sure his mother didn't anticipate that she would need to put anybody other than his father on record as an emergency contact," she said.

"That may well be, Mrs. Rivers, but until your husband allows you to legally adopt the boy, my department won't recognize you as a legal guardian." The older woman seemed very pleased with herself; feeling that she had put this Negro woman in her place. After all, the poor boy's deceased mother was white and she felt a genuine sense of duty to protect the dead woman's interest in this matter.

"I understand your agency has policies, Ms. Dooser, but I don't think my legal standing as a guardian has any bearing on Tatsuya's immediate life," Margarita said, losing some of her patience.

Ms. Dooser didn't seem to see the relevance in what Margarita said. "In any case it's going in my report," the old lady said, looking over Margarita's shoulder at the father and son.

Margarita turned around to see what the old bitch was looking at and what she saw repulsed her. She saw her husband crying. Other than her father, Chemah was the strongest man she had ever known. Seeing him cry when his son needed him the most made her angry. Chemah looked up over Tatsuya's shoulder and saw the two women looking at him. He saw the mocking smile on the old lady's face and the anger in his wife. He didn't care what anyone thought right now, but still wiped his eyes not wanting to alarm his son with such an uncharacteristic display of emotion.

Chemah held Tatsuya at arm's length and looked into his face. Tatsuya's face was tear-stained, but he had a big Kool-Aid smile. Chemah smiled back at him and wiped the streaks away with his thumbs

"Are you alright?" he asked Tatsuya.

The boy's head nodded up and down vigorously. Chemah stood up, took Tatsuya's hand in his own, and stepped to the two women. Despite the looks he saw on each of their faces, he thought they were both beneath his contempt. He spoke to Margarita first. "Is everything taken care of? Do we have to sign anything?" Margarita looked at Ms. Dooser.

"No, Mr. Rivers, there's nothing for you to sign," the old lady answered with some authority. "It's enough that I witness little Tatsuyee gets into his father's hands. If you could just show me some identification so that I can put in my report that you were properly identified, I'm sure you want to take your family home."

Before anyone could answer, Tatsuya spoke. "My name is Tatsuya, not Tatsuyee," he said, looking sternly at the old lady.

She looked down at him and smiled nervously. She looked back at Chemah apologetically. "I'm sorry, I can never get those new African American names right."

"African American names?" Chemah asked confused.

"You know, Tanisha, Quanisha, Shaquida, Tatsuyee," she explained.

"TATSUYA!!" he screamed.

"Yes, yes, Tat-su-ya," Ms. Dooser enunciated, correcting herself.

Chemah reached into his back pocket and took out his wallet, now desperate to show Ms. Dooser his identification before she somehow contaminated his son. After looking at Chemah's ID, she politely handed it back to him. "Well, that's all I needed to see. This young man seems to be in very good hands now."

She then leaned toward Chemah as if she were about to kiss him. "I'm very sorry about your loss, Mr. Rivers." She turned and looked over her shoulder at Margarita. She shot back a smile that only Chemah and a few unfortunate others who had crossed her more than once knew meant trouble.

Ms. Dooser took two steps toward the door before Margarita's voice stopped her. "By the way, Ms. Dooser," she began.

Ms. Dooser turned to face Margarita. "Yes?" she said almost mirroring Margarita's smile.

"I was wondering if you know a Ms. Wiggins?" Margarita asked.

"Ms. Wiggins?" she thought out loud.

"Yes, a Ms. Wanda Wiggins. She also works at the Bureau for Child Welfare."

Ms. Dooser's head popped up as if she'd been slapped in the back of her head. "Well, no I don't know Ms. Wiggins personally. She's the district supervisor. In fact, she's my boss' superior." The smile had come off of Ms. Dooser's face.

"Is that right? Your boss' superior? Isn't this a small world? Just the other day Wanda called me and accused me of not keeping in touch with her. She loves to hear when her people are doing a good job," Margarita said, walking toward the now withering older lady. "I think I'll call her tonight and tell her what a help you were to Mr. Rivers and me. I'm sure she'll be interested in how well you perform your duties," Margarita said, allowing her smile to expose her canine teeth liking a grinning wolf.

Chemah hated to see this side of Margarita. It was as if she enjoyed torturing people. "Honey, I think we should get Tatsuya home now," he said, interceding on behalf of Ms. Dooser.

Margarita stopped her advance on the old lady at the sound of her husband's voice. "Yes, we should be going," Margarita said to Ms. Dooser, her smile still that of a predator.

Chemah and Tatsuya had already reached the door and Margarita didn't want to be left behind. Margarita took two steps toward her husband and stepson, then turned back to Ms. Dooser. "When I talk to Wanda tonight I'll be sure to mention your little problem with pronouncing 'Black' names. I'm sure she'll find a way to help you resolve it."

By the time Margarita turned back to walk out the door, Chemah was nowhere in sight. Margarita felt a slight panic at being left behind. As she rushed through the door, she bumped into the sargeant carrying a cup of coffee. He was able to keep the coffee from spilling onto Margarita.

"I'm sorry, Ms. Rivers," he said, keeping the dripping cup away from Margarita. She ignored him and rushed down the corridor trying to catch up to Chemah and Tatsuya. Margarita reached them at the staircase. Captain Forrest was waiting at the bottom of the stairs.

"Detective, when you get a chance tomorrow I'd like you to stop back here, and have a talk with the detectives in charge of the investigation," he said.

"No problem, sir. I'll be back in the morning," Chemah said.

"There's no rush, son," the captain said. "Call Detective Masserette tomorrow and find out what time you two can talk."

"Yes, sir," Chemah responded and let go of Tatsuya's hand to shake the captain's. After shaking Chemah's hand, he turned toward Margarita and leaned his head forward to kiss her on the cheek.

"It was good seeing you again, Margarita. Don't be such a stranger."

Chemah was taken by surprise. He had not realized that Margarita and the Captain were friends. When they walked out of the precinct, Chemah led Tatsuya toward the Jaguar. He had seen Margarita's car on the way into the precinct and now walked toward it in silence. As he approached the "Jag," Margarita activated the remote car alarm and opened the door locks. *Beep wop!* The noise it made startled Tatsuya. Chemah smiled down at his son, reassuring him that everything was all right. Chemah opened the back door for Tatsuya and helped him put his seatbelt on.

When he stood up again, Margarita offered him the car keys. "You feel like driving?" she said, tossing Chemah the keys before he could answer.

"Sure." He caught the keys easily and walking around to the driver's side. As Chemah and Margarita passed each other in front of the Jag, Chemah caught Margarita's hand in his and gently turned her to face him. "Thank you for being there for Tatsuya," he said softly.

"You know I love that little boy," Margarita said, kissing Chemah gently on the lips.

"I know, but still you didn't have to," Chemah said, glancing at Tatsuya through the windshield.

Margarita followed Chemah's eyes. "When are you going to tell him?" she asked.

Chemah looked back at her. "I think he already knows."

She looked puzzled. "How could he know?"

Chemah shrugged his shoulders. "Genetics. We have a kind of inherited insight. Some things we just know. It's probably the same instinct that makes me a good detective." Chemah sighed. "Let's get him home. We've all had a long day," he said, looking strangely into her eyes.

Margarita went to the passenger side and sat feeling that her life was finally going in the right direction again. She turned around and smiled at Tatsuya. She could see that he was still a little shaken. "We're going home now, baby."

Tatsuya wiped away a tear that had not quite fallen from his right eye and spoke very evenly. "I'm not a baby."

Chapter 16

FOR THE LOVE OF GOD MAN, WHAT HAVE YOU DONE?

Chemah had taken care of all of the funeral arrangements. After breaking the devastating news to Nairobi's father via a long distance phone call, he'd asked permission to make the proper accommodations. Nairobi's father seemed to know all about Chemah. "You have my blessing to do whatever you think is appropriate," Mr. Kimble had said. "My daughter had a lot of faith in you, and I always trusted her judgment. Of course I'll pay for it all."

"That won't be necessary, Mr. Kimble," Chemah said. "I can take care of that, too."

"I'm sure you could, Chemah, but you must allow an old man his dignity," Mr. Kimble had insisted. "I saved up money for what I thought would be her wedding. It belongs to her. It should be used for her last occasion."

Chemah did not have the heart to argue with the elderly man whose voice he could hear cracking under the strain of emotion on the other side of the country. Nairobi had no siblings. Chemah knew she had been the old man's last blood relative. "You're absolutely right, Mr. Kimble," Chemah had said feeling the sting of the old man's words. The two men talked further and Mr. Kimble took on the responsibility of calling other family members to attend the funeral. After he'd hung up, Chemah wondered if it was his imagination or had the old man accused him of not marrying his daughter.

The funeral was a small gathering as Nairobi did not have a lot of living relatives. A large group of her co-workers attended and gave her father their condolences.

The Catholic priest who ministered the service did his best but could not capture the essence of Nairobi's short life.

Chemah was a pillar of strength to all who were in bereavement during the ceremony. He gave out tissues to those who cried. Allowed multiple persons to cry on his shoulder, and through it all held back his own tears. He wanted to be an example to his son of how a man comported himself in times of crisis. Margarita was proud of how her husband handled the situation. She knew the codes Chemah lived by, and resolved in her mind that he was honoring his son by honoring his son's mother. It was one of the reasons she had married this man. While Chemah did what he thought was right, Margarita did her duty as his wife and managed his son. She tried to answer all the questions that the boy had about death and what had happened to his mother, but found that she herself did not have all the answers. She wished it was all over when the pallbearers lifted the coffin and carried it out to the hearse.

Tatsuya asked her, "Is my mommy going to heaven now?"

Margarita had lost her own mother, but she was an adult when it happened. She still bore the pain of her mother's memory. She lied to Tatsuya to avoid the other questions that would be asked by a five-year-old who was faced with adult truths. "Yes, your mommy is going to heaven now," she said, holding back her own tears. Tatsuya took her hand and had to pull her to follow the casket out to the waiting cars.

At the cemetery Chemah couldn't hold it together anymore. He held his son's hand and wept uncontrollably. Margarita was on his left side still acting the part of the dutiful wife. She was embarrassed at her husband's display of emotion, and felt a revulsion to him that was multiplied three times to what she felt when she first saw him cry over Nairobi's death at the precinct. This was not the man she married. If this was the true Chemah coming out after all these years, then she had been a fool. She had changed her true nature so that the man she wanted would always be satisfied. *But if this is what he is,* she thought, *then I don't have the man I thought I had; shit, I could just do me, if it's like that.*

After some final farewells, Margarita was the one who led her husband and new son back to the car. It was in the car where she came to terms with the fact that everyone had moments of weakness. She had been struggling with a few of her own, she thought. Maybe she wouldn't fight them so hard anymore.

Chapter 17
FOLLOW MY LEAD, IT AIN'T FAR

Two months after Nairobi's death, Tatsuya began having nightmares. Before the first scream could finish vibrating throughout the house, Chemah would jump out of his bed and rush into Tatsuya's room, followed closely by Margarita. Chemah would always find Tatsuya sitting straight up in his bed shaking, with sweat forming on his forehead and his upper lip.

The first few nights this occurred Chemah would ask him what he was dreaming about. Tatsuya's only response was to shake even more violently, until Chemah held him closely in his arms and rocked him back to sleep. During Tatsuya's violent trembling, Margarita would look on feeling helpless that she could do nothing for the little boy. Chemah had never seen her look so tenderly at anyone as she did when Tatsuya was in anguish during these nights. Chemah noticed Margarita's pain at the boy's slightest discomfort and it was heartwarming. On the nights when Tatsuya awoke screaming, Margarita and Chemah would stay up for hours after he fell back to sleep talking about what could be causing the nightmares.

On these nights they would discuss Tatsuya's education and his after-school activities along with their general future with him on a full-time and permanent basis. During one of these talks, Margarita suggested that Tatsuya could benefit from having some of his old and familiar belongings that were left in his mother's apartment.

Since Nairobi's death, Chemah had not gone back to Nairobi's apartment, and he didn't think it was a healthy thing for Tatsuya to have to go back there either.

That's why he had bought Tatsuya everything new to replace anything he might have left behind. Any time Tatsuya mentioned something he needed, Chemah would go out immediately and buy a replacement.

The only time Chemah had considered going back to the apartment was during the onset of the investigation into Nairobi's death. The cause of death was deemed to be accidental. The forensic specialists hypothesized that she had somehow lost her foot in the living room causing her to slip and strike her head against the table. They thought that, had she gotten immediate medical attention, she might have lived, but unfortunately she had not been discovered until many hours later. Chemah was only privileged to this information because he was familiar with the lead detective in the case.

He had processed the information he was given concerning the case over and over in his mind and could only come up with one conclusion. He knew that somehow Nairobi's boyfriend was responsible for her death. As a detective Chemah knew it would be hard to determine if Nairobi had been pushed down or if she had actually slipped. The investigation had revealed her boyfriend's fingerprints and hair samples throughout the apartment. This was not enough to make him a suspect. Nonetheless, his phone number was found in the address book in Nairobi's bedroom and he was called in to the station house under the pretense that he had some outstanding warrant. He'd tried to explain that it must've been some kind of mistake and Masserette insisted that he come in and "clear the matter up."

It was a common ploy cops used to get suspects to come in on their own volition. This guy fell for it hook, line and sinker. Once in the precinct John was told the real reason that he was there. The boyfriend had seemed genuinely distraught when he was informed that Nairobi was deceased. Chemah had watched the interview tapes with Masserette.

The man had cried and asked how it had happened. When Masserette had implied that maybe he could shed some light on that particular subject, the boyfriend had panicked. "You think I did it?" he said, pushing his chair away from the table. "I didn't kill her. I loved her. I would never hurt her. The one that you should be talking to is that Rastafarian ex-boyfriend of hers. He was over her house a while back causing some trouble, and I had to put him in his place."

As Chemah watched the tapes over and over, he got madder and madder hearing this man's words. He knew that this man could hurt her and had hurt her before. He had been a witness to one such incident, and as he watched the interview he recounted the story to Masserette who believed him without question.

Nairobi's rent had been paid up a year in advance with money she had inherited when her mother died. Her father had come from Florida for the funeral and left the keys to Nairobi's apartment with Chemah; explaining that he would be back in a few months to settle her affairs. He had told Chemah how Nairobi had spoken so highly of him, and how she knew Chemah would be a great father. Now here he was about to enter Nairobi's apartment for the first time in months and he wondered if he had done everything that he could during the investigation.

Chemah entered the apartment and flicked on the light switch to his immediate right. The light didn't come on, so he tried it again flicking it back and forth repeatedly. When the light still didn't work, he decided to just follow the sunlight that snuck down the long hall and coming through the living room window. Chemah had only been to the apartment a few times but he felt as if he knew his way around. He stopped in the doorway that led into the living room and looked over the books that lined the wall. It made him smile when he thought of how he and Nairobi had spent a whole afternoon and evening talking on the couch.

He managed to pull himself away from the entrance to the living room before he started to feel the tears running down his face. He absently wiped at his eyes as he walked toward Tatsuya's old room. Chemah knew what he was looking for and he thought he knew where to find it. It was Tatsuya's teddy bear. He had brought the thing with him every time he had come over for the weekend. As there was no light to turn on, he found himself feeling around the bed for the furry toy. After about a minute of futile searching, he got off the bed and went to the window to pull up the shade. *I should've done this when I first came in the room,* he thought.

The morning sun lit the room as well as a one-hundred-watt light bulb. Chemah could see the entire room clearly now, but the teddy bear was nowhere in sight. Chemah's first instinct was to look under the bed, and it was right on point. The bear must have fallen under the bed that last morning when Tatsuya had prepared for school. He was sure Tatsuya would not have placed him there on purpose. Chemah reached under the bed and pulled the bear out. Margarita thought that Tatsuya was getting too old for a teddy bear and Chemah agreed with her. The only reasoning that he had for getting the bear back to Tatsuya was that it might alleviate some of his nightmares. Chemah didn't know why, but he felt better himself, now that he had the bear in his possession. Now that he had it, he was in a rush to get out of the apartment. He felt he was somehow intruding on someone's privacy.

As he turned the key in the lock, the sound of the cylinder grinding into place made the hair on his arms stand up straight. He'd found that his senses were working at peak efficiency lately. He was in detective mode. It's what made him good at what he did. He pulled the key out of the lock slowly as if not to disturb any spirits or memories he was attempting to leave behind in the otherwise vacant apartment. Some of the memories would turn bitter anyway, he thought.

As he got into his car he tossed the bear onto the passenger seat. Chemah chuckled to himself as he thought to buckle the bear into the seat. Instead, he just leaned over and sat the bear upright. As Chemah attempted to adjust the bear so that it didn't fall over again he noticed a stain on the back of bear's head. At first glance, he thought it was a food stain, but on closer inspection he realized it was a dried spot of blood. He'd seen and removed enough dried blood stains to know this one had been here at least two months. He dismissed the thought after a moment, wondering how Tatsuya might have cut himself.

Chemah drove toward home thinking of how much more attracted he was to Margarita the past couple of months. She had somehow softened since Tatsuya had come to live with them. He noticed how much more softly she spoke to everyone around, especially when Tatsuya was present. Their lovemaking was tender now and she didn't seem to mind that he didn't cum every time they were in each other's arms.

As he traveled back uptown via Broadway, he spotted a Korean fruit stand and grocery store with flowers out front. He decided to pull over and buy Margarita a dozen roses which were her favorite flowers. Chemah saw the bunch he wanted and pointed them out to the Mexican young man who was minding the front of the store. The man handed Chemah the white roses that he picked, and Chemah went into the store to pay the ten dollars for them. Chemah wasn't thrifty, but he was glad that he wasn't paying flower shop prices for the roses. He didn't especially like roses. The red ones always reminded him of the color blood turned when it spilled onto a sidewalk. For whatever reason, Margarita seemed to always keep them around the house.

As Chemah got closer to his home, his instincts told him he was missing something. Something was tickling at the back of his mind. Whenever he described this instinctive feeling to other detectives he worked with, he described it as a thought that tugged and gnawed and crawled through his mind until it reached his frontal lobes. Chemah finally figured out what it was that was bothering him. He had helped Tatsuya bathe that first night that Tatsuya came to live with him. It was the night that Nairobi had died. The night was so vivid in his mind that he could not have forgotten any part of it if he tried. He didn't remember a Band-Aid on any part of Tatsuya. And more importantly he didn't see any cuts on Tatsuya's hands, and he was sure this cut was from a grown person's finger. *Probably from a fingertip,* he thought, tracing the pattern of the blotted blood in his mind's eye.

He was a block away from his home when he decided to pull over and remove the dried blood from the teddy bear. The first thing he did when he purchased this new BMW was to put a portable forensic kit in the trunk. He'd begun carrying one when he first became a detective. Most detectives didn't carry a kit but it was his expertise and he liked to be prepared for all contingencies. Chemah took his time, carefully scraping the dried blood from the bear's neck and into a small clear plastic container.

When he finished, he took the time to examine the bear further for any hair samples or other foreign matter. Satisfied that there was nothing else he could glean from the bear, he put the portable forensic kit back in his trunk and got behind the steering wheel again. He propped the bear back up in a sitting position in the passenger seat, and stared down at it for a second. Something else was bothering him; he couldn't figure out what and the bear just wasn't talking.

Chemah put the car into gear and slowly pulled out of the parking space. Two minutes later he was in front of his own home, trying to park his BMW behind Margarita's Jaguar. It took him two tries before he could get into the spot. He had to park really close to the Jag in order to fit into the space. Margarita would have a fit when she saw how close he was to her car. She would scream at anyone who parked too close to her precious car. After one particular incident with one of their neighbors, he had suggested to her that maybe she should park at one of the parking garages in the area. She had gotten pissed. "What do you expect me to do? Take a cab to my car?" she had asked. Chemah didn't bother answering her, or offering any further suggestions. Hopefully she would be in a good mood when she came out to her car in the morning and he wouldn't have to hear any shit.

Chemah became so preoccupied with what Margarita would say when she saw his car in the morning that he got all the way to the front door before he realized that he'd forgotten the stuffed toy in the car. He walked back to the car and opened the locks with the remote when he was still twenty feet away from it. He reached the passenger door and opened it. He had to lunge for the teddy bear as he pulled the door, not realizing that the toy was propped against the door. He saved the bear from hitting the dirty street. He smiled and talked to the bear as he headed back toward the house. "You owe me now," he said to the bear.

As if on cue the bear gave up another gift. It startled Chemah at first because he hadn't thought of it. But, as he looked into the bear's eyes, he could see a fingerprint on the right one. Chemah walked back to the car and went into his trunk. This time he pulled a plain brown paper bag out of his portable forensic kit and put the bear inside. He then took a larger clear plastic bag and put the bag holding the bear inside of that. He could try to get a fingerprint out of the eye right now he imagined, but thought better of it as he knew that his friends at the lab would have a better chance of getting a complete print. Chemah knew there was a likelihood that the blood on the bear would be Tatsuya's, and the chances of the fingerprint on the bear being Tatsuya's was also very high. It was only his instincts that told him otherwise.

He started back to the house considering how he would build a case against Nairobi's boyfriend once he had this blood as evidence. Even if he could prove that the fingerprint on the teddy's eye belonged to Nairobi's boyfriend, how could he prove that it was put there on the day that Nairobi died? The day that he claimed he hadn't seen her. *First things first,* he thought as he pushed his key into the lock of his home.

He walked through the door and into the living room. Chemah knew Margarita would be waiting. She saw that his hands were empty and asked the inevitable question. "Did you get the teddy bear?" she asked.

"I couldn't find it," Chemah lied. "'I got all the way there, but when I got into the apartment all the lights were out. I couldn't see a thing. I should've remembered to bring a flashlight. I'll probably go back tomorrow."

"I still say he's too old for that thing," Margarita started to preach again.

Chemah didn't feel like arguing. "Listen, he'll be without it again tonight. Let's see how he does. Who knows? Maybe the teddy bear isn't what he needs. We'll see."

Chemah knew he could get all the information that he needed from the teddy bear by tomorrow afternoon. Tomorrow night Tatsuya would have the bear. He could decide if he was too old for it, Chemah thought. "Where's Tatsuya now?"

"He's watching TV in the family room."

"I thought we agreed that he wasn't going to be watching TV after seven o'clock on a school night."

Margarita looked up from the book she was reading. "Technically, he's not watching television. He asked if he could watch that *Harry Potter* DVD that you bought him, and I said yes, if all his homework was correct."

Chemah shook his head. "You're going to spoil the shit out of that kid," he said, pretending to be worn out.

At that moment, Tatsuya came running into the room, and flung himself at his father. Chemah turned fluidly and caught Tatsuya easily lifting him over his head, pretending that he was going to drop him. It had become a game that Tatsuya started from the day that he moved in. He had marveled at how his father always knew what was going on around him. Chemah was proud that his son was perceptive enough to notice that his instincts and reflexes were slightly more heightened than most other people's. Tatsuya was now always trying to sneak up on him, and Chemah looked forward to it every evening when he got home. Tatsuya laughed almost hysterically as his father held him in the air tickling him. Chemah put him on the ground and kissed the top of his head.

"How did you know, Daddy? How did you know?" Tatsuya asked excitedly.

"I could hear the air in the room move when you tried to stop breathing," Chemah said to him in his most sage voice. Tatsuya cocked his head to the side, trying hard to listen to the air in the room move. Chemah found it hard to keep a straight face. He almost laughed out loud as he looked down at the little boy. Of course he couldn't hear the air move, but he always gave his son a mystical answer when he asked those kinds of questions. He didn't think it would hurt him to think his father was superhuman for a little while longer.

Margarita looked at them and went back to her book. She had learned that these moments were theirs and theirs alone. For a second she thought to dispute what Chemah was saying, then she looked at her husband and thought, *Shit, the things I've seen him do, who am I to say he can't hear the air move?* She continued reading her book. She'd get her turn later when it was time to go to bed.

Chapter 18
Elementary, Watson, elementary

Chemah's partner at the lab had taken the dried blood sample taken from the teddy bear and did every analysis he could. The blood was AB negative; it was pretty common but it wasn't Tatsuya's blood type which was O, the same as Chemah's. Chemah pulled the file on Nairobi's autopsy report just to be sure it wasn't her blood. He found out that her blood was O positive, the same as his and Tatsuya's. He smiled at the irony that they were both the same blood type, and he had somehow missed out on the opportunity to have a soul mate. He had learned to love Margarita, but she was definitely not his soul mate.

Chemah pulled up all the files on John Stallings. They had found out the first time he was brought in for questioning that he had an arrest history. It was a juvenile charge and the file was supposed to be sealed, but that was never the case when a murder was being investigated. It was a minor assault charge and he had never been in trouble again.

John Stallings was a stockbroker and apparently a pretty good one. He lived on the Upper West Side quite near where Nairobi had resided. Mr. Stallings had never been married, and was thirty two years old. His biography didn't fit the text-book murderer, but if there was one thing that Chemah had learned during his time as a homicide detective was that no one ever fit the textbook description.

Chemah pulled up a copy of John Stallings' driver's license and found that he had listed himself as having an A-positive blood type. *It had to be wrong,* Chemah thought. Chemah pulled up John's juvie file again. It was probable that if he spent the weekend in custody that they had done a medical on him. He found what he was looking for, and almost threw up when he saw that the file and the driver's license information was the same. He had been sure that he would be able to link that dried blood to John. Still, there was the fingerprint. He knew the fingerprint wouldn't be enough to put John in the house on the day of the murder, but he would work with it until he found another angle. He'd have to wait for his boy at the lab to confirm his suspicions.

At two o'clock on the dot, the phone rang at his desk. Chemah picked the phone up on the first ring. "Detective Rivers, how can I help you?"

"Hey, Chemah, Rob here, I got what you wanted," the voice on the other line answered. "Do you want to here the good news first or the bad news?"

"Give me what you've got, Rob," Chemah said, crossing his fingers. "I got the fingerprint off of the eye perfectly," the lab tech boasted. "It definitely does not belong to a child. It's much too large. And it definitely does not belong to the deceased."

"Does it belong to John Stallings?" Chemah asked, no longer able to contain himself.

"That's the bad news," the voice on Chemah's phone answered. "I knew you'd want to know, so I checked it against his prints. It was a no-go. I figured while I was at it I'd check the FBI fingerprint database and find out who it belongs to. Unfortunately, whoever that fingerprint belongs to, doesn't have a criminal record—at least not in the United States. I'm sorry I couldn't be of any more help."

Chemah was disheartened, but didn't let on. "I knew it was a long shot, Rob. Thanks for everything anyway."

"Hey listen, anything else you need, just give me a shoutout."

"Thanks, man."

"Peace, Bro." After hanging up the phone he decided to call Rob back. "Hey, Rob, I almost forgot, Brother. I'm going to need that teddy bear back."

"I figured you might. You want to come by and pick that up or do you want me to send it by the next pony going your way?" It was the interdepartmental mailing system to be used only for official business.

"Nah, I'll come get it. I'll pick it up on my way home."

"Good, maybe you can show me some more of that shit you do so well."

"Some of that shit?" Chemah asked.

"Yeah, man, that shit you taught me the last time worked. I showed it to my thirteen-year-old son, and he isn't getting his ass kicked in school anymore."

"Alright, man, we'll work out for a minute."

It reminded him that tonight he and Tatsuya were supposed to go to karate class. It was perfect timing. He needed something to get his mind off of this case anyway. It was time to put Nairobi's memory to rest.

Chapter 19
IF THAT CAP FITS, WEAR IT

Margarita was happier than she had been in a long while. She had the husband that she'd always wanted and although she had desired more than one child, at least now she wasn't childless. Tatsuya was growing accustomed to being in the house with her and Chemah.

It had been at least a month since he had a nightmare. Chemah had brought home his teddy bear, and the night screaming had stopped immediately. She wasn't fond of the idea of Tatsuya having that stuffed bear. She still thought he was too old for it, but at the same time, she hated to see him in such agony every night. Margarita always envisioned that she would raise strong, proud children. She hated to see weakness in this child that was now hers. She believed it was a reflection of what she was. In any case she would let it slide for a while longer.

She was packing her briefcase to head home when Kat knocked on the door to her office. "Come in," she said loudly. The only one who ever knocked on her office door was Kat. Everyone else always called her on the phone or e-mailed her to make sure she wasn't too busy to be disturbed. Kat walked into her office looking as confident as she always did when she had news that no one else had. She walked over to the love seat on the far side of Margarita's office and plunked her fat ass down in the middle of it. Swinging her legs in one smooth motion, she put her feet up on the couch and supported her head with both hands laced behind her neck. "So when were you going to tell me the big news?"

"What big news?" Margarita asked.

"Don't front on me. I already know the symptoms."

"Would you mind giving me a lesson in ebonics and explain what you just said?"

"I'm saying, you don't have to act as if you don't know what I'm talking about. I already know what's going on."

"You know what's going on, huh?" Margarita asked, sitting back down in her chair. "Do me a favor, Kat. Explain to me what it is that you know, because I don't know what the fuck you're talking about."

Kat sat back up on the love seat and crossed her legs over in a more ladylike fashion. "I just got a call from Sheila down at the Mayor's office. The talk down there is that you're going to be appointed the new Commissioner of Community Affairs."

Margarita's first inclination was to laugh at Kat, but she knew that Kat's information sources were seldom wrong. "Now why the hell would I want to be a commissioner in this city? I make more money now than any of them do."

"Maybe for the power and the prestige, and for the fact that all those little dicks in city hall owe you for helping them get there," Kat said out the side of her mouth. "Anyway you don't need the money anymore. You probably have a million dollars stashed by now," she added.

"Don't need money anymore? Who do you know that has enough money, Kat?"

"I know for damn sure that it's not me."

"There was some talk about something like this a long time ago when I was working on the mayor's campaign," Margarita explained. "That was three years ago. After everyone got elected all the promises and well-wishes were forgotten. That's just the way things go during election time. You learn to dodge the bull-shit and keep stepping."

Kat wasn't convinced by Margarita's tough words. "Marge, you cannot pass up an opportunity like this." Margarita hated to be called Marge. Kat knew it, and only did it to tease her into admitting the truth.

"I didn't say I wouldn't consider it. I'm just not holding my breath waiting for someone to ask me."

"The phone call should be coming in any minute," Kat said. "Sheila said her boss had her type out the offer fifteen minutes ago. You're a partner here now, so you have this money still coming in. It's not a conflict of interest because you're not being elected into a position so you'll have both incomes. Just, please take me with you. Give me a title or some shit. I need to make some extra dough, too."

Margarita frowned at Kat's insinuation that she was not looking out for her already when the intercom buzzed and her secretary's voice came on. "Ms. Rivers, you have a call from the deputy mayor's office on line two."

Both women stared at each for a long moment before Kat said, "Well, go on and pick the phone up. Girl, I'm gonna go and pack my shit."

"Shush, let me take the phone call and hear what they have to say." Margarita mentally put herself into character before picking up the phone. "Hello, Margarita Rivers speaking. Oh, Bill, how are you? What can I do for you? Well, yes, I heard about Mr. Ritters' retirement. It's sad, such a young man having a heart attack like that. Dinner tonight? Is it important? I'll have to check my schedule; give me a second."

Margarita held the mouth piece to her chest and waited a second before coming back on the phone. "Yes, I have something on the schedule, but I think I can clear it up. Tavern on the Green. Seven o'clock. That's fine, I'll be there."

Margarita hung up the phone looking stunned. "You were right they're going to offer me Ritters' spot. But why me?" Margarita asked out loud.

"What do you mean, why you? You know why. The administration is always being accused of favoring white males. The National League of Women Voters is always attacking them on the fact that there are no female commissioners in the administration. With you they kill two birds with one stone. And add that to the fact that you know every aspiring politician's dirt. No one is going to question your appointment," Kat surmised.

"You know, for a girl from the p-jays you certainly know your shit," Margarita complimented her in their usual teasing fashion.

"I know," Kat said. "I think I've been hanging around your ass too long. So what are you going to tell him?"

"I don't know. I've got so many things going on in my life right now. Tatsuya needs me more and more. And Chemah and I are like honeymooners again. I don't want to lose any of that. On the other hand, I've been working toward this my whole life. It could be the beginning of another career for me. I think maybe I should discuss this with Chemah first," Margarita said.

She hadn't seen Chemah in two days. She knew he was working on an important case and was working round the clock. She had assured him that she would mind Tatsuya. The thought reminded her. "I have to call the sitter and tell her she's going to have to stay late with Tatsuya. I'll have to rush home and pick him up from the after-school program a little earlier if I'm going to make this dinner meeting."

Margarita was rushing out of the door to catch a cab uptown when she was stopped by Kat again.

"Don't rush anywhere yet, girl. I called a car for you. It'll be here in two minutes."

Margarita tried to rush out again. "Don't bother; I'll just catch a cab."

Kat stopped her again. "You're not going to catch a cab during rush hour, and besides, it's Kenny's car service and he's sending a limo for you to use the whole night."

Margarita stopped to think for a second. Kat was right. "Thanks, Kat."

"No problem. There's the car now," she said, pointing behind Margarita at a shiny black stretch limousine. Margarita was used to traveling in style, but she hated drawing too much attention to herself.

"Damn, isn't that a bit much, Kat?" Margarita exclaimed.

"I don't think so. You've just been playing with the big dogs, but now you rolling with them. You've got to let them know you don't really need them. Then they'll want you even more."

Margarita knew Kat was right. It was a strategy she had to explain to her own clients time and again. Kat had picked up some of her savvy after all. She walked toward the car and the driver came rushing around to her side to open the door before she could reach it. As she sat down and the door closed behind her, one thought crossed her mind. "Hey, I can get used to this." The car wheels started moving and she began to relax.

Chapter 20

YOU BETTER COME WHEN I CALL YOU

Margarita didn't know if Chemah would be home when she got there. He had been working very hard recently and never knew when he'd be home. He thanked her every day for helping out with Tatsuya. She was always a little insulted by this thankfulness as he presumed that it was not her responsibility to take care of Tatsuya because she was not his mother. She needed to speak with him about that.

It was midnight, she realized, as she opened the door to her brownstone and saw the clock sitting on the mantle. She knew Chemah was home. The babysitter would have greeted her at the door or would have been watching television in the living room, if she were still around.

She headed upstairs toward the bedroom and almost wished Chemah were asleep. That would give her time to think of a way to tell him that she had already accepted the position as Commissioner of Community Affairs for the city. It wouldn't be official until another two weeks when she was sworn in, but the announcement would be made to the press tomorrow at a press conference at City Hall.

She had called an emergency meeting with her partners at the consulting firm, after her dinner meeting with the deputy mayor. They had all agreed that her acceptance of this new position would only enhance their winning reputation. The partners were sure that their business would double after the appointment was made, and were almost as excited by the move as she was. Tomorrow she would have to start interviewing for an assistant to help with duties she would be unable to perform for the firm. She had so many things on her plate now, she knew something would have to give.

The door to her bedroom was open. Chemah was lying on the bed fully clothed except for his shoes, which were tossed carelessly on the side of the bed. He was awake and he smiled generously at her as she came through the door. "Hey, hon, you're still awake," Margarita said.

Chemah sat up in the bed, still smiling as if his lips were permanently fixed in that position. "So how did it go?" he asked.

Margarita looked at him quizzically. "You know? How do you know?"

"Kat called to find out how your meeting went. A few well-placed questions, a couple of veiled threats. Any rookie detective could have gotten it out of her," Chemah said, maintaining his shit-eating grin. He climbed onto his knees and leaned over the bed to hug Margarita. "Baby, I'm so proud of you. I know you've wanted something like this for a long time."

Margarita was taken aback by his attitude. She thought he would be upset by her decision to take the position. "I wanted to talk to you about it first, but they needed me to make a decision about it right away. I thought I'd just say yes to get the process going and then come home and talk to you. That way if you and I agreed on it, the ball would already be rolling, and I could start getting everything in place to make it happen."

"I think it's a good decision. Have you decided what you're going to do about the consulting firm?"

"I'm going to stay on as a partner. I'll hire someone to do the day-to-day work, and I'll act as a consultant in all the major decisions. That way I stay in touch with everything that's going on in case I decide I don't like working for the city."

"You seem to have all the answers," Chemah said, exhaling deeply. His concern was starting to show.

"I know what you're thinking, so you might as well say it out loud."

"I don't know what you're talking about," Chemah said in a mocking haughty tone. They had started to become friends again within the last few months and part of that friendship was a consistent teasing and mimicking of each other's more noticeable characteristics.

"You're worried that I won't have time for Tatsuya now that he and I are getting a little closer, and that he'll feel displaced again because he's already lost the love of the most important female in his life. That's right, isn't it?"

Before Chemah could respond, Margarita started talking again. "I've got it all figured out. I'll get up every morning at seven o'clock sharp. I'll make him breakfast. We'll sit and talk, then I'll drive him to school. I'll make sure we talk about interesting things on the way to school, and make sure he knows I still love him dearly. At least two days out of the week I'll pick him up from the after-school program myself and on those days we'll always pick up a special dessert just for him. Of course on the weekends I'll always be free to do the things that he wants to do, unless I have extra work that I have to take care of on someone's campaign. In this case I'll make other arrangements for him where he won't be bored. So there," she said out of breath from talking so fast in one inhale.

"I guess you've thought of everything," Chemah said, settling back against the pillows on the bed. "Have you deduced anything else, Sherlock?"

"Let me think," Margarita said, tapping her finger to her chin as she walked toward him. "I'd say that maybe by the size of the lump in your pants right now, Tatsuya isn't the only one that might be missing me," she said, reaching for the length of thickness that was going down Chemah's leg. Their lovemaking had been very good lately. Margarita was never pressed for him to cum anymore.

He'd been working almost 'round the clock for the last four days and he'd barely touch the pillow before it was time for him to return to work. Touching his wife had been out of the question. However, tonight was different. He'd spent the whole day thinking about being in some pussy. His intention was to come home and make sure that Tatsuya got to bed early, so that he would have time to seduce his wife. When he got home he was disappointed to find the babysitter there, and that his wife would be out late.

When Margarita touched his dick he knew it would be a long night. She bent her head and started kissing the outline of his dickhead right through his jeans.

In response Chemah stroked the top of her head. He allowed his fingers to go through her long soft hair lazily, as someone might do to a cat relaxing on their lap. Chemah was relaxing so much as he felt the heat of her lips press through the fabric of his pants that he didn't realize his zipper had come down and his pants button had been opened. Margarita reached into the opening that his zipper had exposed, and tugged sharply to bring his hardness out into the open. Margarita's lips hovered over the increasingly swelling helmet of his dick as she paused for a moment and looked into Chemah's eyes.

Chemah knew what she wanted. It was a recent fetish that she had developed. Chemah carefully clasped his hand around the hair that began at the nape of Margarita's neck. After a hard tug and a moan that escaped Margarita's lips, he let go of her hair deciding to enjoy the tension that was building between them. The look in Margarita's eyes told him when it was time to touch her again.

This time Chemah placed his hand on the top of her head and stroked down firmly until the palm of his hand came to the ends of her hair, making it into a thick black rope. While continuing to look into her eyes, he began to wind her hair around his hand until his hand was once again at the nape of her neck. Without warning he made his hand into a fist causing Margarita's head to snap back in pain. He could hear her breath quickening as he lowered his mouth to kiss her forehead. Margarita was still poised above his dick as if waiting for a signal from Chemah, but Chemah was drawing out the moment; savoring the power that no one else had over her.

Sex with Margarita had always been different than the sex he'd had with women before he met her. She was always the aggressor and would match Chemah stroke for stroke whenever he tried to fuck the bravado out of her. After the first year they were together Chemah had stopped trying to dictate his sexual preferences. He just allowed Margarita to lead him wherever her appetites took them.

So far the sex was never boring, but she never gave up being in charge. That is, up until recently. Margarita had become a submissive overnight. The one time, years earlier, when he had handcuffed her and fucked her had not gone well. She had allowed him to do what he wanted but it was obvious that she hadn't enjoyed the moment as much as he did. Now, she not only allowed him to do whatever he wanted, but she wouldn't do anything unless he forced her. It was as if she were enjoying being punished for something only she knew she did wrong.

Chemah had tried to question her a couple of months ago about the change in their sex roles and she had only said, "Isn't that what you always wanted? I'm just trying to give you what you want." Chemah didn't buy that answer, but wasn't about to antagonize her into changing back to her old ways. He was going to enjoy it while it lasted.

Right now he was tightening his grip on her hair and enjoying the torn emotions he saw in her eyes. She was forcing herself not to take his dick in her mouth until he ordered it. "You want it?" Chemah whispered to her. Margarita attempted to nod her head yes in answer but Chemah had too strong a hold on her hair. He tightened his grip even more when she tried to move. "I want to hear you say it."

"I want it," she acquiesced.

"You want what?" he demanded.

"Your dick," Margarita answered obediently. This was the moment that Chemah was waiting for. He reaffirmed the grip he had on her hair and forcefully brought her head down on his dick. Margarita gagged for a second, but continued to allow his dick to slide down her throat. After a few seconds, Chemah felt Margarita trembling around his dick. He knew she was cumming, as she did every time they played this game. He almost came watching her orgasm, but was able to control himself at the most crucial moment. *Better to hold back*, he thought. *She's going to want more.* Chemah was enjoying himself as he indulged himself in his wife's mouth. It hadn't occurred to him yet that even in his new role as the dominant one, Margarita still controlled when he came.

Chapter 21
Do you, Ma

The first few weeks after Margarita's appointment as Commissioner of Community Affairs went by without a hitch. Margarita had gotten the okay to bring her own people in positions she thought would be key in making her appointment a success. She'd initially had some reservations about bringing Kat aboard as Deputy Commissioner, but later scolded herself at being surprised at Kat's ability. Kat had not only held her own in the last few weeks, but had also held her down a few times when she was not in her office, and things could have taken a turn for the worse.

In front of the rest of the staff Kat was a model of efficiency and professionalism. It was only when they were by themselves that Kat would go into homegirl mode. Throughout their years of working with each other, Margarita had continuously chastised Kat about showing her ass in front of white folks. Apparently Kat had been listening to her after all. Right now Kat was chastising her about delegating responsibility. "Fuck, Marge, you could have at least let me known that you were going to be out of the office half of the damn day. You know I got your back every time, but you've got to let a sister know what's going on so that I can at least appear to be making intelligent decisions."

"I know I should have let you know about the Upper East Side money allocation, but I thought I'd be back in time to deal with it," Margarita lied. "I got caught up in a lunch meeting with the partners about some new business and I forgot the time. I'm sorry," Margarita said, trying to end the discussion.

Kat folded her arms and sat at the edge of Margarita's desk. "Are we still friends, or am I just the help now?" Kat asked.

"Of course you're still my girl. Who else could I trust to have my back in this camp?" Whenever Margarita tried to act like she was down, it came off sounding fake. Kat knew she was lying.

"Margarita, if something is wrong, you can tell me," she said sincerely. "I called the midtown offices looking for you. Jane told me all the partners were there. Everybody but you. I work for you; you don't have to lie to me, but as a friend I want you to know if anything is wrong, I'm here for you."

Margarita felt bad about lying to Kat, especially since she had been caught in the lie. "I can't explain it now, Kat," she said, her eyes telling more than her mouth, "but I can assure you that everything is alright and I won't leave you hanging anymore."

This seemed to satisfy Kat, who was actually more concerned about Margarita's welfare than the job. She knew that she had handled the situation just as Margarita would have. "Okay, Marge," she said, smiling at Margarita to let her know that they were still partners. "I have to get ready to leave now, Marcus is taking me to the theater tonight, and he hates it when I keep him waiting."

"Who's Marcus?" Margarita asked, trying to keep the girl talk going.

"We'll talk about him tomorrow. You can tell me your shit and I'll tell you mine." She walked out the door turning to wink at Margarita before closing the door behind her. Margarita was glad that Kat had left satisfied with the answers she had given her. Margarita on the other hand was not satisfied with her own answers. She knew she was slipping. If Kat was able to detect that something was wrong, Margarita wondered why Chemah hadn't noticed it yet.

Her meetings with Captain Dennis Forrest were becoming a dilemma. After the first time she had slept with him she knew that she had complete control of the situation. It was simply a power move she rationalized; pushing the real reason she had begun sleeping with him to the back of her mind.

The problem now was that he was claiming to be in love with her and was demanding more and more of her time. She had to think of a way to slow down or stop his demands completely. Margarita never thought that it was possible she would have sex with a white man. She had never been attracted to any before Dennis Forrest. She remembered when she had made the decision to sleep with him—how it excited her to imagine him, this big powerful man who was admired by his peers and all the men at his command begging her to make him orgasm. At that time she had no idea of the power she would be able to exert over him. She guessed that he had not been with too many other Black women.

Later she found out that she had been his first. He had told her how he had been intrigued by her ever since they had first worked together on the mayor's campaign four years before. She had to remind him that he did not work with her, but for her. The fact that his time was volunteered was inconsequential, she had said.

Margarita had arranged for them to have dinner at the W Hotel on Lexington, and unbeknownst to Dennis Forrest, had arranged a room for them through the consulting firm, under the guise of wooing a client. Dennis was surprised when Margarita suggested that they go up to a room that she had arranged. Dennis was used to assuming the role of the leader and found it refreshing that he could relax and let someone else take the reins for a while. He didn't know that Margarita by nature would have it no other way.

When they reached the room, Dennis attempted to take control of the situation again. Margarita had a little trouble opening the door using the key card. "Here, let me try," he said, taking the card from her and sliding it into the door slot. The green light on the lock showed immediately indicating that the lock was open. Dennis pushed the door open.

"Voila," he said, imitating the French maitre d' downstairs at the restaurant. "After you, Madame," he said, making a grand sweeping gesture with his hand through the open door. Margarita smiled at Dennis as she stepped through the door. He took it as a sign of approval. In actuality she was laughing at him, wondering if all white men were this corny when they were trying to get laid.

Margarita was snapped out of her musing when she heard the door close behind her. She was turning around to face Dennis when she was suddenly whipped around by her right shoulder and fell into his waiting arms. Margarita looked up into the eyes of this man she knew other men respected and admired, and could only feel amusement. She almost laughed out loud. The situation was getting cornier and cornier. Dennis' lips were coming down slowly to meet with hers, and she was reminded of Rhett Butler in *Gone With the Wind.*

She stepped into the room. Margarita realized that she had to quickly take control of the situation. She had seen this look of passion in many men and knew that it was a crucial moment when they were willing to do anything to fuck the woman in front of them. "No kissing," she said, putting her hand between her mouth and his before he could come any further. Dennis had a look on his face like she had punched him in the balls.

Before he could say anything else to make matters worse, Margarita took him by the hand and led him toward the king-size bed, which was conveniently located in the center of the suite, facing the balcony.

When she got him to the bed she grabbed him gently by the shoulders urging him to sit at its edge. Dennis looked up at her quietly waiting to see what she would do next. Without saying a word, Margarita slowly got down on her knees in front of him and then bent slowly at the waist. The smile on Dennis' face told the secret his mind thought it was keeping. *I'm going to get my cock sucked.* But instead of undoing his belt or his zipper, Margarita reached down and started to untie his shoe laces. The look on Dennis' face changed slightly as Margarita removed his shoes and socks but it was not an unhappy look. After removing his footwear, Margarita remained on her knees in front of him as she began to undo his tie. She removed it quickly and then changed her pace as she began to slowly unbutton his shirt. Without looking directly down she had already glimpsed his dick twitching in his pants.

Margarita slowed her pace even more when she noted the painful look of longing on his face. She wanted that look to last a little longer. Margarita freed the last button from its hole and firmly tugged the shirt free from his shoulders exposing a Fruit of the Loom white cotton T-shirt. She could see the wisps of hair stemming from his chest come out of the top of the T-shirt, and wondered if fucking him was going to be like fucking a gorilla.

Margarita steeled herself, resolving that she had already gone this far and pulled the T-shirt over his head. She wasn't grossed out like she thought she'd be. Dennis' body was surprisingly hard. He was sporting a six-pack that was sparsely outlined by the peach fuzz that was growing directly down the middle of his stomach. His chest was well muscled and not nearly as hairy as she had first thought. Dennis looked for approval in her eyes and found none. Her poker face was in full effect.

Margarita tossed the T-shirt to the side and finally reached for the belt that would undo his pants and her fidelity. Margarita slid the unbuckled end of the belt out of the loop and held it firmly. Looking Dennis in the eyes again, she yanked the belt hard to her left causing the buckle pin to come out of its hole. Dennis had restrained himself from shouting in pain, but was not able to stop a slight grimace from telling the pain Margarita was causing in his side.

Margarita smiled wickedly and let go of the belt allowing Dennis to breathe easy again. Margarita undid the snap in the front of his pants with one hand and slid the zipper down without looking down. She nudged Dennis' shoulders, indicating to him that he should lie flat on the bed. When he was reclined, she grabbed his pants at the waist and yanked them off his hips. Dennis tried to help by lifting his hips off the bed but it was unnecessary; Margarita's strength had already prevailed.

After dragging the pants the rest of the way down his legs, she threw them to the side with his T-shirt and shirt. She eyed the white Fruit of the Loom jockey shorts and thought, *Shit, can a pair of underwear be any less sexy?* Her own husband never wore underwear, she was reminded. The sexiness of that she thought was unquestionable. Margarita eyed the bulge in Dennis' underwear and thought it might be slightly smaller than her husband's.

Dennis was still lying on his back, unsure of whether he should sit up again or continue to allow her to lead. He strained his eyes to try to look down at her with his head flat on the bed; he was scared that if he interrupted her she would stop. Margarita attempted to prolong Dennis' agony even longer by toying with the elastic of his jockey shorts before beginning to slowly pull them down.

Margarita could not contain her surprise as she sucked in her breath when she saw the size of the dick underneath the white material. It was easily the biggest dick she had ever seen. What she had assumed was a hardened penis had in actuality been Dennis' dick in its resting state. She knew that when it hardened it would be almost impossible to fit in her mouth. Dennis propped his head up when he heard Margarita's startled inhalation. He saw the surprised look on her face before she could regain her composure. He smiled down at her and then rested his head back on the bed feeling a bit more in control.

Margarita regained her composure, but knew she had lost some ground in the "who's your daddy" department. She saw the dick in front of her lengthening and thickening into a frightening instrument, and knew she had to do something fast or she would end up impaled and at his mercy. Margarita got up off her knees and stood with her hands on her hips. "Slide up to the middle of the bed," she told him.

"Aren't you going to take your clothes off, too?" he asked, as he did what he was told.

"In a minute," she said, crawling onto the bed after him. "I just want to enjoy you like this for a while." Margarita lay on top of him and began by kissing his neck. She spent a few minutes there, and felt herself get excited as the mammoth dick continuously poked her in the belly. Eventually she started to make her way down to his chest, gently kissing and nibbling along the way. Margarita got down to his rock-hard stomach and felt the hardness poking her in the chest. Margarita was unwilling to admit to herself that she was turned on by what was going on. She could feel the wetness sliding down her own leg, but refused to acknowledge it. When she reached his pubic area, she grasped his penis to keep it from beating her in the face, as Dennis flexed it uncontrollably every time she kissed near it. She had no intention of going down on him so soon. She wanted him to become so excited that he couldn't help prematurely ejaculating. She knew he would then be apologetic and feel indebted to her. She knew a man's nature, she thought.

The compulsion to suck on the fat dick that she was barely containing with one hand was making her dizzy. Margarita stopped kissing around his pubic area and told him to turn over. Dennis had been confused, and hadn't immediately complied with her request. "Huh, what for?" he asked.

"Shhhh, trust me," Margarita reassured him. Dennis started to turn over and stopped abruptly when he felt Margarita's tongue on the head of his dick. After the slow lick Margarita allowed Dennis to lie on his stomach.

"Jeeezus, why did you stop?" he asked as he settled on his stomach. Margarita had been unable to resist tasting the huge penis, and now fought the yearning to go back to it. She knew Dennis would do whatever she said at this point. *God, it tastes like honey,* she thought. To Dennis she said simply, "Don't worry, baby, it's only going to get better."

She immediately started kissing the back of his neck, going slowly until she reached his buttocks. Dennis had been shocked when she started kissing down the crack of his ass, but really started to protest when she parted his cheeks and started licking his anus. "What are you doing?" he said, unsure if he really wanted her to stop. Margarita ignored his protest, and he quickly forgot that he had complained at all. He was enjoying the feeling that she was giving him more than any sexual experience he could ever remember.

Chemah had never allowed Margarita to go this far with him. She knew the reason he had refused was that it gave a woman too much power over you after the act was over. She was counting on this hypothesis and was planning to take it further than she had ever considered. When she pulled her lips away from his ass, Dennis almost protested again. Margarita flipped him back over on his back and speared her mouth with his dick.

Dennis was enjoying the feeling that Margarita was giving him when he felt her finger creep into the crack of his ass. He was going to protest again, but didn't want the feeling that her mouth was giving him to stop. When Margarita inserted her finger into his ass coupled with his penis in her mouth, it seemed like a natural progression of pleasure for him.

When Margarita realized that he was no longer protesting, but rather enjoying it, she began thrusting her finger into him deeper and faster, never once letting up the vacuuming with her mouth. Margarita hadn't thought that he would hold out as long as he did. When she realized that he was holding back his orgasm, she inserted another finger in his ass and pounded him even harder. Margarita released his penis from her mouth to allow herself to be able to talk.

"Cum, motherfucker." Margarita gasped as she inserted yet a third finger into his ass. Dennis' breath caught in his throat and he feebly protested the new intrusion in his ass with a groan. Margarita rammed her own face down on his groin filling her throat, which oddly had the effect of disabling both of their vocal cords. With a final effort Margarita pushed her mouth down to meet Dennis' pubic hair and felt his resolve to hold back his orgasm give as his balls grazed her chin. As she felt his testicles jump, she pulled her mouth back so that his seed didn't go straight down her throat. Dennis' dick jerked a few times and he made a mewling bitch sound that almost made Margarita laugh. "Eeeeeeah, eeeeeah, eeeeeah!" Dennis screamed.

White boys sure cum funny, Margarita thought, experiencing her first taste of white-boy sperm. Margarita didn't swallow the fluid; she allowed it to seep out from the sides of her mouth as fast as he released it from his dick head. She was so excited by the copious amount she was causing him to release that she thought she might come.

When it was over Dennis seemed embarrassed that he had enjoyed the experience so much. He immediately got up and went to the shower. When he came out, he began getting dressed as if nothing extraordinary had happened. Margarita gave him a knowing look. They both knew he had enjoyed the new experience more than he would ever admit. When faced with it he became a little red-faced and tried to carry on a normal conversation.

Margarita sat in her office now remembering the whole scenario and all the times that she had met him after. Dennis never pressed her for normal sex. He followed her lead every time they were together. She had created the same dependence on sex with her that she had developed with all the other men she had used before her marriage to Chemah. Today she had fucked Dennis with three fingers while she sucked his dick, all the while plotting how she was going to finally get rid of him.

Her main concern now was that Chemah never find out that she was being unfaithful to him. He wouldn't understand that she had done it all for him and Tatsuya. She also knew that her logic for being unfaithful could only be understood by another woman. She didn't have another female that she could confide in. She would do anything to ensure that he didn't find out.

Chapter 22
De Hardest Hard

Chemah decided that it was time he and his family take a vacation. Margarita was working on two separate careers and it was taking its toll on her. She had begun to miss appointments and was once even late picking Tatsuya up from school. After his failure in proving that Nairobi's ex-boyfriend had something to do with her death, he felt that he needed a cleansing of his own soul. He wanted to be the best husband and father that he could be, but he knew that if he didn't let go of Nairobi's memory, his life with Margarita and Tatsuya would never be fulfilling.

Chemah had traveled to a few places in the Caribbean, but had never been to the islands where his grandfather was from: Trinidad and Tobago.

He had already checked with both of Margarita's secretaries to ensure that she had no appointments that could not be cancelled or postponed for a week. The tickets he bought were triple the price they would have been had he thought to arrange the trip six months earlier. Chemah was looking forward to getting away from the cold weather. New York in February was not for the faint of heart. When he spoke to his mother, she suggested that he needed to replenish his fighting spirit with nourishment from his ancestors.

It happened to be Carnival time in Trinidad and Tobago. It was when the natives celebrated the freedom of the slaves from the sugar plantations. On islands where the class system's unfairness rivaled that of the race wars in the states, it was not uncommon to see a bank president or a CEO drinking and carousing in the streets with those they normally considered their servants. The experience only lasted two days and all the classes took the opportunity to live outside of their normal restraints. Trinidadians always boasted that after you experience your first Carnival, you can't help coming back every year.

Margarita had balked at the first mention of a trip that would take her away from the two offices that she was responsible for, but reconsidered after Chemah suggested that he and Tatsuya would not have as much fun if she did not come along. Chemah had been bluffing. There was no way he would consider taking a trip like this without Margarita. The entire reason for the trip was to recharge the battery of energy that had reignited their marriage a few months ago. Chemah had felt the momentum of that energy waning and wanted to stop its decline before they were at the point where they were not communicating again.

Previously he had accepted that his marriage may not work out and he would have to cut his losses and move on with his life. Now, it was his responsibility to provide Tatsuya with a stable home and he refused to shirk his role in giving his son a normal life.

Margarita was refastening Tatsuya's seatbelt. They were beginning their decent into Piarco International Airport in Trinidad. It was Tatsuya's first flight and like any other child would, he was running up and down the aisles at every opportunity. He was oblivious to the fact that they were in first class. Chemah didn't want to put a leash on him, he was afraid that he would ruin Tatsuya's first vacation.

He still remembered the only vacation he had taken with his parent when he was the same age. He hadn't been allowed to move without his mother's approval. He remembered being trained to look at her first when a neighbor or family member asked if he wanted something to eat. His mother never had to nod yes or no. In fact she would barely look his way at all. It was more like a sideways glance that told him he'd better not move or accept whatever they were offering. He had gotten his fair share of ass whippings before he knew what these looks meant.

Chemah allowed Margarita to rein Tatsuya in whenever it was necessary. Apparently she hadn't been scarred by strict corporal parenting and knew when and how to draw the line with kids. Chemah smiled as he witnessed Tatsuya trying to get over on Margarita, and saw how easily she turned the tables on him. Tatsuya looked at Chemah for support, but Chemah acted busy putting his own seatbelt on. Tatsuya finally settled down and looked out the window until the plane landed.

It was noon when they landed. The pilot had announced that it was eighty-five degrees in Port of Spain, Trinidad. Chemah felt a relief as he guided Tatsuya down the steps that were placed on the side of the plane, allowing them to disembark. He hated the cold that New Yorkers were accustomed to in February, but wasn't looking forward to having his clothing stick to his skin, either. To his pleasure, he felt the cool West Indian tradewinds caress his skin. The air was not stifling, unlike that of an eighty-five-degree day in New York. A beautiful hostess greeted them at the bottom of the steps. Chemah could see all the mixtures of races that had occupied the island in the young woman's face. She extended a hand offering him a cup of rum punch. Chemah took the cup and attempted to use his peripheral vision to get a second look without Margarita noticing

"Shit, I can get used to this," Chemah said under his breath. Margarita heard him and slapped him playfully on the back of the head.

After picking up their luggage, they left the terminal and walked outside to find a man holding a placard that read Rivers. Chemah had prearranged transportation from the airport with the travel agency. Knowing well the reputation for notorious highway men that Trinidad has, he didn't want to subject his family to any more chaos than he had to.

On their way to the Trinidad Hilton hotel, the driver pointed out various sites that he thought the Rivers would find interesting. Chemah paid little attention to him. Instead he just enjoyed the simplicity of the island. He looked at the mountains in the distance freckled with small homes and imagined that the people living in them were happy with their simple existences.

Tatsuya was in awe of all that he had never seen and pointed out the same things that their guide was mentioning. Margarita looked on at all the things that Tatsuya pointed out. She tried to act as excited as he did, but was distressed by some of the things that she saw. There seemed to be people living on the side of the road. Separating the homes from the road was what could only be a garbage dump.

There were children scavenging through the garbage; Margarita only hoped that they were not looking for food.

The driver announced they were nearing Port of Spain and proudly pointed out the city's twin towers. Tatsuya had gone on a school trip to the World Trade Center and knew that they were also called the twin towers. He looked in the direction that the driver was pointing, but was disappointed to see that these twin towers were nothing more than two similar buildings that stood approximately the size of the building that he had lived in with his mother.

He turned around and frowned in Margarita's direction. She in turn shrugged her shoulders to indicate that she also did not understand what the big deal was either.

After a few more minutes, the driver turned right off the highway and started his way down a two-way street. Chemah looked out the car window, trying to locate a street sign. As the car crossed another road, he saw a sign that said Cipriani Boulevard.

"We goi'n pas round the Savannah now," the driver announced in an accent that had always sounded to Chemah like a cross between Irish and Spanish. He remembered that his grandfather had had the exact same accent.

Tatsuya didn't seem to be having any trouble understanding the native lingo that he had always found confusing when he was the same age. Chemah remembered constantly asking his mother to interpret what his grandfather had said. When he was eight his grandfather came to stay with them for a whole summer and told Chemah stories about his native island. His description of the land of his birth was so vivid that Chemah almost felt that he had been there himself.

When Chemah heard the driver say that they were about to pass the Savannah, he sat up in his seat. His grandfather had often talked about the Savannah and wonderful horse races he had witnessed there throughout his life.

As they rounded the corner, Chemah, Tatsuya, and Margarita all looked out of the right passenger window. Chemah was confused when the car completed its turn and he saw a makeshift stadium on the outskirts of a vast field. There were hundreds of people milling around preparing tables with food to sell and a vast assortment of crafts. His grandfather had always described the Savannah as an open field filled with many of the plants and flowers that were indigenous to Trinidad.

"What's going on over there?" Chemah asked the driver.

"Dat is Panorama," the driver answered.

Chemah remembered his grandfather describing the meeting of two competing steel-pan bands as a gang war. He had never mentioned there ever being a formal Panorama competition. His grandfather always boasted the fact that the pan was the only instrument that was invented in the twentieth century. His grandfather had not lived to see that the great competition was now held in a stadium.

"That's Panorama?" Chemah asked, sounding confused.

The driver seemed to understand his confusion. "Yeah mon, de competition gettin' bigga and bigga every year. The North stand take up more and more of the Savannah with each competition. I tink one day dey might build someting permanent."

The car passed the temporary structure and Chemah sat back in his seat again. The driver continued to act as a tour guide, pointing out the country's zoo, the most prestigious finishing school for young men, and the most likely place to get coconut water at any time of day or night.

When they finally reached the hotel, Chemah had decided that he would ask the concierge to get him tickets to the Panorama event.

They all followed the bellhop to the elevator and up to the suite Chemah had rented. Tatsuya had seen the entrance to the pool the minute the car had come to a stop at the driveway and was hopping up and down, begging to go.

"Daddy, can we go to the pool first? Please, please, please," Tatsuya begged.

"Shouldn't we go to our room and change into our bathing suits first?" Chemah said teasingly.

Tatsuya didn't realize he was being teased. "We can change over there," he said, pointing to the bathroom in the lobby.

"I don't think so, son. Let's go upstairs and change, and then we'll come down by the pool and get something to eat. I'm sure there'll still be plenty of time for swimming after that," Chemah assured him.

"Margarita, can you take Tatsuya upstairs to change?" he said, kissing her on the cheek. "I have to talk to the concierge a minute."

"Don't take too long, baby. I don't know how long I'll be able to hold Tatsuya back from diving from the balcony into the pool."

Margarita and Tatsuya followed the bellhop into the elevator, and Chemah went to the concierge's desk. Ten minutes later, Chemah was strutting into his hotel suite, holding three tickets in his hand. "I've got the tickets," he announced.

"The tickets to what?" Margarita asked.

"*Panorama!*" Chemah said, holding the tickets in front of him as if he had just won tickets to Willie Wonka's chocolate factory. "The concierge keeps extra tickets for hotel guests, and we got the last ones for this afternoon."

"But I wanted to go swimming," Tatsuya whined.

"We can still go swimming for an hour and get something to eat. The show doesn't start 'til four o'clock. That gives us plenty of time to do what we all want to do," Chemah explained.

Tatsuya didn't care what the plan was as long as he went to the pool. Margarita was indifferent. She was only along for the ride. Wherever her man was taking her, that's where she belonged. She had convinced herself that this was the philosophy she had to internalize if her marriage was going to survive.

✸✸✸

Margarita was actually enjoying the pan show. The music was rhythmic and alive. She found herself jumping along with all of the native people that had come to see their favorite bands. Chemah had Tatsuya on his shoulders so that his little man wouldn't miss any of the performances. After a while the crowd got so hyped by the music that they started stomping and dancing with one another. Somehow the wave of people pushed Margarita further and further away from her husband and new son. Chemah and Margarita kept an eye on each from afar. They were careful not to lose sight of each other, lest they get separated.

Margarita had noticed the hard-backed men who were pressing in on all sides of her before they became aware there was an available woman to grind on. The other women in the crowd didn't seem to mind the men that were grinding on them, and it didn't seem any different than what goes on in the New York City club scene to Margarita.

Chemah was startled to see Margarita dancing with two men at the same time, but when she waved to him through the crowd, he knew she had everything under control. She was laughing and swinging her arms to the beat. The crowd was so tightly packed that it would take Chemah at least five minutes to get to Margarita who was approximately twenty yards away. It was turning dark but the heat of the day was still with them. Margarita felt the sweat trickle between her breasts and down toward her navel. The man who was behind her was sadistically grinding his dick into her ass. If she had been in a club in New York, she would have pushed this character off. Now, she was thinking, "When in Rome do as the Romans do."

She was enjoying the man's hardness and was thinking about how she was going to tear Chemah up tonight, when she felt the man behind her sneak his hand into her pants waist. She started to make a scene but wondered how far this man would dare to go.

When she was single six years ago, she would make it a point to get freaky while she was on vacation. Making sure she got it all out of her system before she came back to her real world. She was married now and shouldn't be thinking this way.

She knew that no one could see what this man was doing to her. The crowd and the darkness were taking care of that. Her only concern was what would happen if Chemah came closer and inspected what was going on. She wasn't big on promiscuity but her recent change in roles with Chemah made her want to test her ability to manipulate men. She made her decision when the man reached her pubic mound. Margarita pushed her ass back against the man's pelvis, letting him know that it was all right to continue. She took the hands of the man in front of her and placed them on her shoulders so that they wouldn't interfere with what the man behind her was doing down below.

She waved at Chemah one more time. This time both he and Tatsuya waved back. When they turned their attention back to the pan performance, Margarita started to go to work. Her task was simple, she thought—make the man behind her come before he could reach her pussy. She reached behind her and felt for the man's zipper. She ripped the zipper down and shoved her hand into the man's pants. The dick she felt was not as big as she thought she had felt through his pants. The man instinctively attempted to reach deeper into Margarita's pants. Margarita jerked real hard on his dick a few times and the hard-backed man behind her stopped moving. She could tell he was trying to keep himself from coming. She jerked hard a few more times and felt warm fluid flow over her fingers. She removed her hand and wiped it against the man's pants leg. When the man behind her tried to continue his hand's descent into her pants, she grabbed him by the wrist and yanked him away from her waist.

Margarita made a disgusted face so that the man in front of her thought he had done something wrong. She then whipped around so that they both stood staring at the man standing behind her trying to tuck in the limp wet penis hanging out of his pants.

The man who was dancing in front of Margarita found this amusing. He raised his voice so that those in their immediate area heard him. "Boy, if ya don tink you ca handle real wuman, you should na be doin tings a real mon do."

Others in the crowd saw what was going on and started to laugh and point at the man trying to compose himself.

Margarita took this opportunity to escape into the crowd and head toward Tatsuya and Chemah. When she reached Chemah, she put her arm around his waist and squeezed him gently. Chemah looked down at her and smiled.

"You finish getting your freak on, baby?" he said. "I thought we'd lost you to the natives."

"You couldn't lose me if you tried," Margarita said, squeezing him harder.

This is just what she needed to get her head back together, Chemah thought.

✷✷✷

After five days in Trinidad, Chemah started to think that the island was played out. He had two days left before it was time to head back to New York and he was already itching to return. Margarita and Tatsuya were down by the pool again; he was all pooled out. He was waiting for Tatsuya to come back up to the suite. He thought he would take him down to the hotel gym and teach him the beginning of a new kata. When Margarita and Tatsuya came into the suite, they were both smiling.

"Alright, you two, what's up?" Chemah asked.

"We have a surprise for you," Tatsuya said.

Chemah looked to Margarita for a better answer.

She was ready. "It's just that you've been bending over backward trying to make sure that Tatsuya and I are having a good time, and you haven't done anything that you like. I was asking around downstairs and it turns out that a couple of the young men are involved in a martial arts club, and they've agreed to take you with them to one of their training sessions. I told them that you were a master and they didn't seem that impressed when I said you were from New York, but they said they wanted to meet you."

Chemah couldn't suppress a smile.

"They're waiting for you in a car downstairs right now. Leave now and you could still have a good time on your vacation," Margarita said, pushing him toward the door.

"Aren't you guys going to come along?" Chemah asked.

"We're going back down to the pool," Tatsuya answered, while helping to push his father toward the door. "I met a new friend, and we're going to have swim races."

Margarita shrugged her shoulders, as if she had already given in to him.

"Okay, okay, I'm leaving," Chemah said. "Don't have dinner without me" were his final words as they pushed him out the door.

Tatsuya had to use the bathroom and Margarita changed into a more revealing bathing suit. She had gotten into the spirit, after the first day of vacation when she made the man come at Panorama. Since then, she had made a different stranger come each day. She decided that any sexual thing she did with another man during her vacation did not count as infidelity. Besides, she wasn't actually having sex with anyone, she was just having a little fun.

‡‡‡

The whole family was tired. They were all on the plane sleeping off their exhaustion. Chemah could understand why his son was so tired. Tatsuya swam either in the pool or at Maracas Beach each day that they had spent in Trinidad. Chemah was surprised to find out that he could swim very well.

When the three of them reached the pool on the first day, Tatsuya had scared the shit out of both him and Margarita by jetting off in front of them and flinging himself into the deep end of the Hilton pool. Chemah ran to the edge and almost dove in after him before realizing that Tatsuya was gently treading water and calling for him to come in and play.

"Jump in, Daddy, jump in. Last one in is a rotten egg," he called out to him.

Chemah looked down at him trying to decide whether to jump in the cool-looking water when Margarita rushed up to his side.

"Did you know that boy could swim?" she said, looking down at Tatsuya in astonishment.

Chemah shook his head no without looking at Margarita. Had he looked at her, the smile on his face would probably have withered. She looked like she could eat a box of three-inch sheetrock nails.

"Well, maybe it's a good thing we took this vacation, then," Margarita said. "No telling what else we'll find out this week," she said sarcastically.

She started to walk toward the lounge chairs, but changed her mind and turned back to Chemah, who was watching Tatsuya glide through the glistening water. Chemah looked the part of the proud papa. "I'll be the rotten egg," Margarita said as she attempted to push Chemah into the water.

In a split second, Chemah sidestepped Margarita's hand and used her own momentum to propel her out over the pool. She landed next to Tatsuya and went under quickly. When Margarita came to the surface, she was thrashing wildly.

She still had her robe on and was finding it hard to keep afloat. Chemah looked down at her and they both started laughing simultaneously.

"The rotten egg will be over by the lounge chairs having a drink," he said to her, and started walking toward the bar.

Margarita struggled to get the robe off and threw it to the pool's edge. *I might as well enjoy the water now that my hair is fucked up,* she thought as she swam toward Tatsuya.

I swear that bastard should be in a ninja movie, she thought proudly of her husband.

✳✳✳

Chemah looked over at his sleeping wife and wished that there were a middle seat in first class so that he could rest his head on her shoulder. He touched the bump hidden under his locks and winced at the memory that the bump brought back. His head was still pounding from his last visit to the Gayelle.

The Gayelle was the name of the arena that was used for stick fighting in Trinidad. When the young men whom Margarita had met by the pool invited him to their martial arts class, he took it for granted that it would be karate or kung fu. When they got to the class, Chemah was introduced to the instructor as a martial arts master from the States.

Chemah had bowed graciously and the instructor held out his hand and extended it to Chemah. He took the older gentleman's hand and felt a little sheepish at his own sense of self-importance. The older man introduced himself with only his first name.

"Welcome, youthman, my name is Michael," he said, grinning broadly.

The class started very soon after Chemah's introduction to the rest of the class. Chemah's previous experience with a sword allowed him to work out with the senior and most experienced stick fighters in the class. It was evident after the first hour passed that Chemah's skill with the stick was far superior than that of any of the students in the class.

Chemah and Michael talked a while after the class was over. Michael had never been to the States and showed a curiosity for experiences outside of his country that Chemah found refreshing. After talking for what seemed like hours, Michael apologized to Chemah for having to leave.

"Chemah, would you like to come back tomorrow and help me teach the class?"

"I don't know if I would be of any use in teaching one of your classes, Michael," Chemah said in a lame attempt to be humble.

"Respect, youthman, but my students, like others in this country, are easily impressed by anyone that speaks with a Yankee accent," Michael said with a genuine smile. "Just your presence here would make for a more than ordinary class."

Chemah recognized the calm certainty with which the man spoke. He reminded Chemah in many ways of Grandmaster Sam McGee.

"I'll see you tomorrow," Chemah said, getting up and bowing to Michael before walking out of the door. Michael waved to him from the doorway. The simple gesture moved Chemah to wave back a little more enthusiastically than would have been acceptable for him back in New York.

When Chemah reached the class the next day, there were twice as many students as the day before. The word had gotten around that a martial arts master from the States would be teaching the class and every errant student who had not been training for months had somehow found their way to class. Michael informed the class that Chemah would be doing the warm-up and asked that they give him their attention.

It was soon evident that this last request was not necessary as every student hung on each word that Chemah uttered and carried out all of his instructions as if God himself had put in the request. When Chemah felt the class was warmed up, he signaled to Michael that the class was ready. Michael shrugged and continued flipping through the magazine that was in his lap. Chemah had not anticipated teaching a whole class by himself, but found that these students were very open to the concepts of Harlem Goju and found himself easily walking around to each student and instructing while Michael looked on from the border of the gayelle.

Chemah was invited back again the day before his last day on the island. He knew he wouldn't be able to come to the gayelle on his last day on the island and wanted to extend a sincere thanks to Michael for allowing him to experience this part of the culture. When Chemah reached the gayelle, he found that Michael had invited students to the class that he had not seen previously. Michael explained that he had invited some of his more advanced students who didn't come to the class as often due to time constraints. When Michael introduced Chemah to these students, he explained that he did not want them to miss out on an opportunity to experience martial arts from another teacher's perspective.

Chemah was allowed to teach this advanced class and all the students seemed to be thankful for the experience until one of them asked him if his techniques were better than their teacher's. Chemah didn't want to show disrespect to Michael but also wanted to be honest with the student.

"I'd say that we're different," Chemah explained. "I don't think you could say that one martial art is better than another."

Michael was standing on the outskirts of the class, listening. His students looked to him for another answer but he just nodded his approval at Chemah's explanation. At the end of the class when all of Michael's students were gone, Michael suggested to Chemah that they could both learn from one another if they worked out alone for a while. Chemah was already warmed up from working out with the students so he suggested to Michael that he may want to stretch.

"We'll go slow at first," Michael said. "I'll warm up like dat."

Chemah and Michael picked up the sticks that they used for fighting and started moving around each other in a fashion that resembled a dance. Chemah seemed to be performing an Asian dance and Michael seemed to be miming a Trinidadian folk dance. The movement of their sticks striking each other quickly went from slow motion to a blur that was hard to follow with the naked eye. Michael was feinting and jabbing at Chemah in between strikes so quickly that it took all of Chemah's speed to avoid getting hit. Michael stepped sideways suddenly, holding his stick in the middle and letting it rest against his leg in a position that let Chemah know he was no longer a threat. He ducked his head demurely, just enough to avoid Chemah's swinging stick.

"Alright now," Michael said, taking a slow deep breath. "I'm ready."

Chemah stopped his stick in mid-swing and stepped back in wonderment of what the elder man was talking about. Chemah already had used every bit of his skill to avoid being hit by this elderly gentleman and he was now being informed that he had only been warming the man up. Chemah took an on-guard posture, remembering the first lesson of martial arts: never take your eyes off of your opponent.

Chemah watched the older man lift his stick above his head and begin to twirl it like a drum majorette. Chemah quickly found that he had almost no defense for Michael's attacks. Each one of Michael's swift and brutal attacks was contested by Chemah, only to end with Michael picking Chemah up from the floor and apologizing for a bruise or bump on Chemah's body.

After approximately half an hour worth of foot in his ass, Chemah was ready to call it a day. Michael saved Chemah further embarrassment when he announced that he was tired and they should end their training session. Michael wiped nonexistent sweat from his brow and walked into his office to retrieve two bottles of water from the small refrigerator he kept there.

"Youthman, dat is de bes workout ah ever had in a long time," he said as he handed Chemah a bottle of water.

Chemah took a long pull on the bottle before attempting any sort of communication. After downing two-thirds of it in one swallow, he turned to Michael and asked, "How bad was I?"

Michael looked at him curiously and asked, "Did you practice with me to find out how good or bad you are?"

Chemah shook his head no as he realized that he had brought shame upon himself and his karate system. The question he'd asked was impertinent and showed his lack of humility. The only ones that ever made him feel this way were his own two instructors.

"You made the very classic mistake of underestimating your opponent, Chemah," Michael counseled him. "Didn't you think that I would be proficient at the very thing I've dedicated my life to teaching?"

"I don't mean to be disrespectful, Michael, but I guess I was judging you by your students," Chemah confided. Michael presented his gentle smile.

"Youthman, you should know better than to judge a teacher by his students. Are all the students in your dojo as good as you are?"

Chemah grinned sheepishly as he shook his head no.

"I didn't tink so, boy," Michael said in his thick accent. "You say yah people are from dis island, youthman. That makes you brethren to all de people of dis island. You should not tink small of dem lest you tink little of ya'self."

Chemah knew what Michael meant when he imparted those pearls of wisdom to him. He accentuated them by giving him the lumps on his head that he was now tenderly rubbing as he admired his beautiful wife who had started snoring in the airplane seat next to him.

Chemah looked at his son who had fallen asleep while leaning on his left shoulder leaving a trail of saliva that had soaked through Chemah's shirt.

Tatsuya and Margarita had really bonded on this trip. They had all gained a great deal of release from the pressure of their normal lives in New York, Chemah thought. He himself had come to recognize another part of his psyche that he never believed existed.

Chemah was eager to share the most recent lesson he had learned with his son, but as he looked over at the sleeping child, he realized that what he really wanted was to keep his son from making the same mistakes that he had made. As he adjusted his son's head to move it away from his saliva-soaked sleeve, he decided that Tatsuya had already had a share of reality-altering lessons that a boy his age should not be entitled to.

"You've had enough reality to last you a couple more years," he whispered near the top of his head as he leaned down to kiss him.

Chemah took a second look at his wife and tried to come to terms with the discontent he felt in his core. He knew other men found her attractive. How could they not? She had always maintained her figure. Her ass was as shapely as Jennifer Lopez's, without any cellulite. And when she could hide her contempt for men, she had the face of a Madonna.

Her looks were not the issue. He just couldn't fake loving her anymore. He barely even liked her. As he considered their relationship from the beginning, it became clearer to him that he had expected a love for her to just blossom out of nowhere. She was the type of woman that he had always pictured himself with. So when she had appeared almost out of nowhere and showed so much interest in him, he had thought that eventually he would fall in love with her. Those feelings had never appeared, but somehow he got caught up in a bunch of moments and wound up married.

Before his son came to live with them, he had come close to deciding that he could no longer remain married to Margarita. His loveless marriage had turned into an ever tightening tourniquet that threatened to cut off all the emotion he had ever felt for anyone else in his life. Ironically, just when Chemah was about to make the decision to leave Margarita, Tatsuya came into his life and everything changed. In the back of his mind, he thought that Margarita would not accept Tatsuya into their home and he would use that as the reason for leaving her.

When Nairobi died, Margarita stepped right in as the doting surrogate mother. It was obvious to Chemah that Tatsuya needed Margarita more than he needed to feel the love of a woman that he could love in return. Chemah was willing to give up any chance of happiness for the rest of his life so that his son could have the love of a mother again. *So what if I never know the tender love of a woman again?* he thought as he stared down the cleavage of his wife's blouse.

He was married to a woman that loved to fuck. *That should be enough for any man,* he thought, resigning himself to his plight as he reclined the airplane seat to finally work on his own comfort.

Not everybody in a happy family gets to be happy, he decided, as he closed his eyes and settled in for the rest of the long monotonous trip.

Chapter 23

WHAT'S A FOUR-LETTER WORD FOR LOVE?

Margarita's phone had been ringing off the hook since she arrived at her office on the Monday morning after returning from her family trip to Trinidad. She never allowed her administrative assistant to answer her phone unless she wasn't in the office. A quick look at the caller ID told her that her finger-fucked friend Captain Dennis Forrest was on the line. It was the third time he had called in the last two hours but she hadn't been ready to talk to him until she finished making all of the arrangements for their next rendezvous. She'd just hung up with the W Hotel and had reserved her usual suite for Tuesday and Wednesday.

"Margarita Smith's office, Margarita speaking. How can I help you?" she said, holding the receiver loosely.

"Hey, Marge, Dennis here," the captain said, obviously trying to sound casual.

"Hello, Dennis, I haven't heard from you in a minute," she said, resenting the familiar way he had shortened her name to Marge. "Is everything alright?

"I think maybe that's something I should be asking you," the captain said, still trying to hide his exasperation. "I haven't been able to track you down for three weeks."

"Oh, I had a family emergency and had to go out of town," Margarita said, giving the answer she knew he would construe as, "it's none of your fucking business."

"Oh I see," he said, taking the hint. "I hope everything's okay," he added, trying to get back into her good graces.

"Everything is fine now. When am I going to get to see you?" she said, beating him to the punch.

"Whenever you want," he responded, biting his own lip for allowing himself to sound too eager.

"Well, I can't see you tomorrow, Dennis. I have too much work to catch up on, but how about Wednesday?"

"Wednesday is fine," Dennis said, still not able to keep the excitement out of his voice.

"I'll call the hotel as soon as I get off the phone and see if I can arrange our regular suite."

"That'll be fine. I'll call you back tomorrow and confirm that we're still on," he said, sounding even more needy than before.

"That won't be necessary," she said, making him self-conscious of his eagerness. "I'm sure I'll be able to get the room, but if you feel the need to just talk, you can call me anytime." She had the upper hand now and would not let him give up the role of the submissive.

"Alright, I'll talk to you tomorrow then," Dennis said, reluctantly getting off the phone.

"Alright honey, be good," Margarita said sweetly. Margarita didn't bother hanging up the receiver. She touched the button for her second extension and dialed the phone number of the Wesley detective agency. "Hello, Mr. Wesley, please," she said into the receiver.

The secretary on the other end sounded young and bored. "Who shall I say is calling?"

"Yes, you can tell him Margarita Smith is on the line."

"Mr. Wesley is in a meeting right now," the young voice responded. "Would you like to hold, and I'll see when he'll be available to talk with you?"

"Yes, I'll hold," Margarita said, also sounding bored.

Moments later a gravelly voice came on the line. "Hello, Ms. Smith?" the voice with uncertainty.

"Hello, Mr. Wesley, how have you been?" Margarita began, still using her most sweet voice.

"I'm OK," Mr. Wesley responded in his gravelly voice. He knew better than try to make quaint conversation with this woman.

After a brief silence, Margarita got to the point. " I have a job for you."

"I'm listening," the gravelly voice almost growled.

"I need a set-up like the last time—same place, but this time I want at least three cameras, one in each room. The suite will be available to you tomorrow."

"That's kinda short notice," he said sharply. "It's gonna cost."

"Don't fuck with me, Wesley; can you do it or not?" Margarita said, making the man on the other line wince.

"It'll be taken care of, Ms. Smith," he said, remembering exactly who he was talking to. "And how will you be paying for my services, Ms. Smith?" he said, exaggerating his politeness.

"Bill me, you fucking idiot. How do you think?" Margarita hissed into the phone.

It was a stupid question, the gravelly-voiced man on the line knew, but he had never seen nor heard this woman lose control before, and he did not like to be talked to in that manner. They had done business on several other occasions and money had never been an issue. It wouldn't do to make money an issue now.

"I understand, Ms. Smith." he responded, keeping his tone respectful.

"I'm glad you do," Margarita said, regaining her composure. "On Wednesday at exactly eleven p.m. you can pick up your money at the usual place. After you get your money, you'll be allowed to pick up your equipment. Is that clear?" Margarita waited for a response.

"Very clear."

"Good," Margarita said, returning to her sweet voice. "Have a nice day, Mr. Wesley," she said and hung up the phone.

There was a sharp knock at Margarita's door. Thinking it was her administrative assistant, she absently said, "Enter." Kat entered the room closing the door behind her carefully. "Hey, Miss Kat, since when do you knock on my door?"

Kat smiled broadly, glad that Margarita had noticed this small change in her behavior, then looked sheepish for a moment. She looked back at the closed door and seemed to metamorphose from a businesswoman to a project chick in the time it took for her to turn and face Margarita again. Her posture changed and her hands became animated as she talked. "Shit, since you brought me over here and gave me this new position, I can see why you always complained about me not knocking on your office door before coming in. I swear people just think you have nothing better to do than just talk to them all day. Answering their stupid questions and shit," she said, sucking her teeth.

Margarita missed talking to Kat the way they used to. Since she had brought Kat with her from the firm, they did not have a lot of opportunity to bullshit. Margarita had given her a position with a lot of responsibility and Kat had risen to the occasion.

"Anyway, I was just on my way to drop some kids off at the pool and I thought I'd look in on you and see how your vacation went," Kat said.

Margarita looked at Kat quizzically for a moment before asking, "What kids at what pool are you talking about?"

Kat smiled wickedly. "You know the bathroom." Margarita still looked at her in bewilderment. Kat leaned onto Margarita's desk and looked her dead in the face as she enunciated each word carefully. "I have to take a shit," she said as if she were talking to a person who was hard of hearing.

Margarita rocked back in her seat and laughed while holding her stomach. "Girl, you are sick," Margarita said as she struggled to catch her breath. "Where did you come up with that one?"

"I heard it on some television show," Kat admitted. "I thought it sounded more civilized than 'I gotta shit,' but it appears you are not in touch with the most recent in bourgeois etiquette," she said, tossing her hair back in an exaggerated flair. The two women looked at each other dryly for a second and then both broke up laughing. "Oh, God stop, stop," Kat said, holding her side, "I'm starting to prairie dog."

Margarita couldn't stop laughing, but was able to question Kat in between guffaws. "Wha…wha…what's prairie dog?" she asked unable to catch her breath.

"You know, prairie dogging," Kat tried to explain between deep breaths. "When it pokes its head out of the hole and then back in, out and in, out and in." This information made Margarita laugh even harder. She herself thought she would pee her pants. "Oh, oh, oh, wait, wait," Kat said, still holding her sides. "That was close," she said, standing up straight after a moment. Margarita's laughing had just subsided. "I have a date after work; I can't afford to be shitting my pants at work today," Kat confessed.

"Didn't I tell you to always keep an extra pair of underwear at work?" Margarita jokingly chastised Kat in a motherly tone.

"I'm on my period and already used up the extra underwear I keep for emergencies," Kat said in a matter-of-fact voice. "Damn," she said, holding her crotch. "My pad is soaked and as bad as I have to shit right now one more laugh is going to make it look like I'm keeping peanut butter and jelly sandwiches in my underwear."

"Eeeewww, you are nasty," Margarita said, wrinkling up her face in disgust.

Kat was delighted to know that she could still offend her friend's sensibilities in this way. Kat started toward the door taking short clipped steps, purposely doing the shit walk to keep her friend laughing even after she was gone. "I'll talk to you later." Kat waved and closed the door behind her.

Margarita continued to laugh, glad to have anything take her mind off of the deceitful web that she continued to weave around herself. A sobering thought suddenly crossed Margarita's mind. *Kat knows Dennis Forrest. If he's been calling for the last two weeks, Kat must know about it. She has, after all, been handling all of my phone calls while I was away.* "I wonder why she didn't mention him?" Margarita asked herself. She made a mental note to ask Dennis who he had talked to each time he had called.

Chapter 24

IF IT AIN'T ROUGH, IT AIN'T RIGHT

ednesday couldn't come fast enough for Captain Dennis Forrest. He had been spending so much time in the bathroom playing with himself while Margarita was gone the past two weeks that his wife thought he had a stomach infection and suggested that he see a doctor before he becomes dehydrated. The concierge at the W Hotel recognized him and gave him a knowing nod as he swaggered through the lobby toward the elevator. When the elevator door opened Dennis rushed forward almost crashing into the elderly couple who were attempting to disembark.

"Pardon me," he said, deftly stepping to the side. As they passed he thought he detected the faint aroma of Preparation H. His house had been left reeking of the stuff throughout his wife's pregnancy, and the slightest smell of it was now enough to turn his stomach. Dennis got on the elevator and pressed the button for the twenty-second floor. He popped a rum raisin LifeSaver into his mouth vaguely aware of the lingering smell of medicine that the old couple had left behind. He chewed the LifeSaver, crushing it between his molars so that there would be no evidence of it when the doors opened again. When they did, he hastily swallowed what was left of the LifeSaver and had to consciously stop himself from skipping out of the elevator.

"Stay cool," he cautioned himself aloud as he adjusted his gait in imitation of some kids he'd seen in a music video. When he reached the door he had been in only twice, he knocked sharply twice and stepped back so that when the door opened, his entire form could be viewed from head to toe by the woman whom he found so intoxicating. He had dressed to impress tonight and didn't want any part of his ensemble to go unnoticed.

When the door opened, Margarita stepped just inside the door and leaned against the door frame with her arms folded against her chest taking a moment to appreciate the man who was standing outside the hotel door. Margarita thought he looked like one of the models in her Macy's catalog. Someone who should be wearing an Izod Lacoste shirt with the little alligator on the left side of his chest. Instead he wore a dated tuxedo that was a little snug around the shoulders and slightly high around the ankles. "At least he's not wearing white socks," she almost said out loud. "Mmmm, delicious," Margarita said, licking her lips provocatively. "Come in, you're a little early, but that will just give us more time to spend together," she said, allowing the door to swing open in invitation.

Margarita walked away from the open door giving Dennis an opportunity to view her swaying hips through the translucent Frederick's of Hollywood lingerie adorning her lithe body. Dennis stepped over the threshold of the door and walked in the footprints Margarita's dainty bare feet had embossed in the plush carpeting. Margarita's hips led him into the living area of the suite where he briefly lost sight of them as she stepped behind the bar to fix them both a round of drinks. "Scotch and water, no rocks?" Margarita asked almost sounding as if it were a suggestion rather than a question.

"How did you know?" Dennis asked without really caring how she had known his drink preference. He was still attuned to her hips and his question came instinctively rather than a need to know.

"All of the real men I know drink scotch," she lied as she laced the drink with a very mild sedative. She stirred the drink briskly to dissolve any evidence of the extra ingredient and brought his drink around to the couch where he was now sitting. "Here you are," she said, handing him the tall drink.

"Whoa, are you trying to get me drunk?" Dennis asked, accepting the drink.

"Why, are you afraid I'll take advantage of you, Captain?"

"More like I hope you'll take advantage of me." He snickered. "Cheers," he said, raising his glass to touch with Margarita's.

"Cheers," Margarita said in return, touching her glass to his.

Dennis put the glass to his lips and took a long swallow. "Mmmm. That's very good scotch," he acknowledged.

Margarita smiled up at him. "Thank you, I brought my own supply. I didn't want to chance the hotel not having hundred-year-old scotch."

"Hundred-year-old scotch?" Dennis asked incredulously, bringing the glass up to eye level. "I don't think I've ever had hundred-year-old scotch before. I'm going to savor this," he said, taking a smaller sip this time.

Margarita watched him steadfastly wondering how fast and how much the mickey she had slipped him would take effect. "Why don't we take our drinks into the bedroom?" she said seductively.

With no aplomb Dennis hopped to his feet, almost spilling his drink in his excitement. He looked to one doorway, then another, trying to remember in which direction the master bedroom was. He then realized that he could not remember the layout of the suite. Margarita reached up to Dennis offering him her hand to help her off the couch. "Oh, allow me," he said, gently helping her to her feet. Margarita was surprised by his gentle touch. In their previous encounter, she hadn't paid much attention to his hands. Margarita allowed him to continue to hold her hand as she led him through the living room and into the master bedroom. In the center of the room there was a king-size brass bed.

"They've redecorated the room." Dennis noticed as he came to the foot of the bed. It was covered with a royal-blue satin sheet with five round gold pillows resting against the head.

Dennis tried to take Margarita into his arms, but she warded him off pressing her right hand and her drink into his chest. "Not so fast, Tiger, let's finish our drinks first," she said coyly. Not one to be put off easily, Dennis put his drink to his lips and this time tilted the drink far back chugging it until it was all gone. Dennis pulled the glass away from his lips and Margarita could see he was paying the price for his reckless drinking.

The burning sensation that he was feeling in his throat and belly was clearly expressed in his face. Dennis wiped his watering eyes with his free hand and gasped to catch his breath. "Wooowee, that was smooth," he said, looking for somewhere to put his glass down. Dennis walked over to the table that was near the window and placed the glass more carefully then a sober man would.

Margarita could tell that the extra ingredient she had placed in his drink had started to take effect. When she noticed a slight stagger to Dennis' gait as he walked toward her again, she knew it was time for her to put her plan into effect. Margarita put what was left of her drink down on the side of the bed and motioned for Dennis to come to her.

Dennis fell into Margarita's arms and they rolled onto the huge bed. Margarita maneuvered them so that she was on top. When Dennis pushed his head up in search of a kiss from Margarita, she darted her head forward for a brief and perfunctory touching of their lips. She then started to kiss her way down his body. As she had in the past, she started with his neck and worked her way down to his chest. The process was slow as her lips and tongue had to linger in one area while she fumbled with the task of taking his clothes off. Dennis attempted to help her by undoing a few shirt buttons, but when his hands became unusually heavy to lift, he decided he'd just lie back and savor the sensations that his drink and Margarita's lips were causing him. She had removed his shirt and was kissing his navel and loosening his belt when she looked up to see her handiwork. Dennis was smiling dreamily; his head rocking from side to side like an autistic child in his own world.

Margarita finished undressing Dennis, but by this time he was all but incoherent. The drug that she had given him had done its job well. She stood up and looked down at Dennis to assess how she was going to complete the caper she had started. Margarita was astonished to see that even in a drug-induced state, the man was still sporting a massive erection.

Margarita licked her lips. "Yummmm." She almost bent down to get a good taste. Not one to normally let a dick like this go unlicked, she playfully slapped herself on the wrist. "Bad girl, business first and then we play."

Margarita walked over to the closet where she had left the overnight bag with all the supplies that she would need. She carried the bag to the foot of the bed, then proceeded to undress. When she was totally naked, she reached into the bag for the one thing she would be wearing for the event, a hooded red mask. Margarita hated the claustrophobic feeling she was getting by putting on this mask, but it was a necessary evil. Once the mask was donned, she reached into the bag again and pulled out a remote control.

Her man had placed two cameras in the room facing the bed and had wired them both to this one remote. Margarita pressed the record button and although she knew it was impossible, she thought she could hear the whirring sound of a camera. She had never allowed herself to be filmed in a sexual act, but was intrigued with the idea of acting out her own personal fantasy and having it recorded with the possibility of others viewing it. Never mind that no one would ever know it was her, she still felt giddy.

Margarita's first thought was to bend her head to the task of "sucking that fat dick." To her disappointment the hole that was made in the area designated for her lips to protrude from, did not allow her to open her mouth wide enough to take in Dennis' helmet. In frustration she grasped the shaft with both hands and started to jerk him off as she licked around the head, alternately sticking her tongue into the hole on top to retrieve the sticky clear fluid that was not coming out fast enough to satiate her hunger for it.

Dennis' head continued to loll from side to side, but Margarita doubted that he even knew the source of his own pleasure, as she proceeded to forcibly insert her index finger into his ass. "Now comes the good part," she said, facing the mirror where she knew the camera was hidden behind. She thought some narration might benefit anyone who saw the tape.

Margarita ripped her finger out of Dennis, causing a low moan to be emitted from his half-open mouth. With strength that seemed unusual coming from someone of her stature, she easily rolled Dennis over onto his stomach, careful to point his cock toward his stomach and not his feet, so as not to have it snap off at its base. Dennis' head had rolled along with his body causing his mouth and nose to be facing directly into the mattress. Margarita adjusted his face left, so that he could breathe properly and also be videoed by the other camera in the room.

Margarita reached into the overnight bag again and pulled out two sets of handcuffs and set about extending Dennis' hands above his head and cuffing them to the brass bars attached to the bed. Margarita didn't think that Dennis would be regaining his senses anytime soon but it didn't hurt to take precautions. Besides, the cuffs added an extra nastiness to the act she was about to perform. After taking a second to admire the way she had rendered this huge man helpless, she rummaged in her bag for the last piece of equipment that she would need. Seconds later she pulled out a large dildo attached to a harness. Margarita's mouth was slack and she could feel her salivary glands working overtime as she practically drooled while she attached the device to her hips. She simultaneously watched Dennis' ass go up and down in time with his breathing. When Margarita finished attaching the last strap, she reached for the small canister of Astroglide lubrication that she had brought.

Initially she had intended to take this man's ass with no lubrication at all; in a tribute to all the brothers out there that knew nothing about anal sex and always attempted to take their women's asses with no preparation or regard for their partners.

Feeling magnanimous she applied a healthy amount of lubrication to the phallus artificially attached to her hips and then spread over the entire length using the up and down jerking-off motion of an adolescent young man. Margarita knelt at the foot of the bed and spread Dennis' legs in one quick and violent motion. She saw the prize she was after winking up at her between his fat white ass cheeks and began to creep between his legs using only her knees to propel her forward.

When she finally reached her goal she had to consciously steady her breathing. She knew she was going to enjoy what she was about to do, but the excitement of a sexual act had never taken her breath away as this one. As she positioned the head of the dildo against Dennis' asshole, she took a long deep breath, turned toward the camera, and winked. Margarita plunged the huge phallus into Dennis' ass and probably right into his stomach, she thought, in one fluid motion.

Even in Dennis' drugged state the impact of his ass being opened to its fullest for the first time had taken his breath away. Margarita heard the loud grunt, "uuuuhhh," escape from his slack lips and held the phallus in its new sheath until she was sure that she had not shocked Dennis out of his drugged state. When she was sure that she wasn't going to be thrown off of his back, she gently reached under his stomach searching for the hard fleshy shaft of his cock. When she found it, she began to let her hand glide up and down its length. Her hand still held the residual moisture of the Astroglide and she found her hand moving with the dexterity of a concert pianist.

This extra sensation brought forth a contented mewling sound from Dennis and was a sign to Margarita that she could proceed with the invasion of his ass. Margarita slowly worked the dildo out of Dennis' ass while continuing to play with his dick. When just the head was left in him she paused for a moment, then slowly began her descent back into his asshole.

After approximately three minutes of using the same technique, Margarita noticed an almost imperceptible movement coming from Dennis. He was leaning back into her fake cock on every down stroke. Margarita removed her hand from Dennis' penis and grabbed him by both shoulders in order to give herself more leverage. Margarita picked up the rhythm that she was tattooing into Dennis' ass until she was sure that if she fucked him any harder he'd have to be taken to a hospital when he came, too.

As she was fucking him Margarita found that if she flexed her ass at the last moment of her down stroke, the harness caused the sort of friction in her clitoris that was making her itch to cum. When she came to this realization she began to focus all of her attention on scratching her own itch. The result was that Dennis was getting the phallus rammed higher and higher into his ass. It took Margarita a solid ninety seconds to orgasm once she got the rhythm right. She shuddered and shook for a time before collapsing onto Dennis' back.

In Margarita's frenzy, she had missed the moment that she had been trying to capture. That is, she missed Dennis' imminent orgasm. It wasn't until she reached under his belly to stimulate his penis again that she knew he had already come. Although she missed it, she knew that the cameras had caught the whole scene. Margarita wanted to have more fun with Dennis while he was still unconscious, but for that she would need to take her mask off.

She had gotten all she needed on tape, she thought. Margarita picked up the remote control that she had haphazardly thrown on the bed and pointed it at the two locations where she knew the cameras were hidden. Both times she clicked the power button ensuring that nothing else would be taped. Margarita pulled off her mask and took a deep breath; she was thankful that she could breathe easy again. Margarita rolled Dennis onto his back and saw that his penis was flaccid again. She pouted at the shriveled appendage and bent her head to clean up the mess that she had caused.

Chapter 25
LOOK WHAT YOU DONE DID

Chemah didn't frequent the labs much anymore as lesser detectives were given the chore of taking different samples of evidence down to the lab. It was only by chance that he got the opportunity to see his boy Rob, the lab technician, as he was on his way to the crime scene technology supply division to pick up a supply of evidence bags. "Hey, Chemah, what's up, man?" Rob greeted him, shaking his hand in the fashion that professional black men usually reserve for one another when their white counterparts are not around.

"What's happenin', Rob?" Chemah said, holding his grip on Rob's hand a second longer than was actually customary.

"Nothin', nothin', just a struggling white boy trying to keep his head up." Chemah liked Rob, but never understood why Rob found it necessary to speak like he was straight out of the hood. Chemah knew he wasn't trying to clown blacks. He had visited Rob at his home in the suburbs and found that his two sons (eleven and twelve years old) spoke the same way. His wife was the only one in the house who had spoken plain English to him. His boys had been polite and respectful to Chemah, but mimicked their father in their speech.

"Yo, check it, I was tryna shout you out and let you know 'bout that fingaprint you had me scopin'."

Chemah's awareness was instantly magnified at Rob's words. "You found something?"

"Nah, it was a bust," Rob replied. Chemah's spirit felt spontaneously deflated.

Rob could see the pain in Chemah's face when he gave him the news. "Yeah, I thought we was gonna make somethin' of it, too, but shit, we ain't no ma'fuckin' supa men, nam sayin'?" Rob put his hand up to give Chemah dap.

"Yeah, thanks for trying," Chemah said, reaching out to clasp Rob's hand against his own. Rob wasn't satisfied with what would have been a quick show of appreciation and pulled Chemah to his shoulder and clapped him on his back.

"Man, show a nigga some love, show a nigga some love," Rob said enthusiastically.

Normally Chemah would have been appalled at a white man using the term "nigga" or "nigger" for that matter, but he didn't have the need or desire to strain his and Rob's friendship at this time. "You're a crazy mothafucker," Chemah said as he laughed and pulled away from him.

Rob took this as a term of affection and pounded his chest with his open right hand. "One love, brotha, one love."

"I'll see you later," Chemah said, turning away from Rob. "Call me if anything else comes up."

"Yeah, we still have the blood. That might still turn something up," Rob said skeptically as they started to move away from each other.

"So we're giving up on the fingerprint," Chemah said, still moving away from Rob.

Rob also was walking backward as he spoke. "Yeah man, I was telling you it was a big mistake. It turns out it was your wife's fingerprint the whole time. She must've touched the eye of that teddy bear before you gave it to me," he said matter-of-factly.

Chemah stopped, frozen in time for what seemed like an eternity. When he regained his composure, he turned and started walking toward Rob again. Rob stumbled backward as Chemah came marching toward him. For a second he had the impression that Chemah was going to strike him. "What do you mean it's my wife's fingerprint?" Chemah asked as he approached.

"Just what I said," Rob said, trying to appear undeterred by Chemah's naturally threatening presence. "While you were on vacation, I decided to check the print against the computer bank again, and I came up with a match. I got excited for a second, but when I looked and saw it was your wife's print I knew it was a mistake."

"Why didn't the computer match the prints up before?" Chemah asked.

"Her prints weren't in the banks before," Rob replied, ready for the question. "I checked it all out. Apparently the new job she has working for the city requires that she be printed, and all those prints go up to Albany for a background check. We were lucky to have caught it at all. At least now we know we can give that up and concentrate on the blood."

"Yeah, I guess we can concentrate more on the blood now that we know the print is a dead end," Chemah said, trying not to give anything away.

Rob tried to make a joke of the situation. "Yo, I wasn't gonna say nothing, man, but you fallen off, man, you fallen off. Gettin' your wife's fingerprint and shit. What you gonna do, handcuff her and beat her down next?" Chemah tried to smile at Rob's attempt at humor. "You still my boy, tho, you still my boy," he said, pounding his open hand into his chest again. "Yo, I'm Swayzee, I'll check you. My lady's picking me up with the seeds in a few minutes."

Chemah looked perplexed for a second. "Swayzee? Seeds?" he said out loud.

"Swayzee, Knucka, as in I'm ghost, gone. Seeds, as in fruit of my loins, the boys. Damn, kid, keep up! The brothas are gonna think you ain't down anymore," Rob berated him and turned away, walking down the long hall, and away from where Chemah's life had just been turned inside out.

Chemah had not heard the last part of Rob's admonishment. His legs were already carrying him on a dead run to his car. He was on his way to Margarita's office. He was undecided as to whether he would kill her or allow her to try to explain when he got there.

Chapter 26
Gotcha!

Kat tried to explain to Chemah that she didn't know where Margarita was, but could see with the determination in his face that her boss' husband was not in the mood to play any games. She and Margarita had both seen Chemah for the first time during a martial arts ceremony and it was evident then that he was a cunning and dangerous man. She wanted to protect her girl's privacy, but she was not about to fuck with him. She sensed he was in a particularly dark space and she was making it her business to be as helpful as she could to him.

"I checked the parking garage downstairs; the Jag is still there. How did she leave?" Chemah asked.

"She took the car service," Kat said without hesitation.

"Which one?"

"We only use one. I keep the number right here on speed dial." She gestured toward her phone receiver. Chemah reached over Kat's desk not waiting for permission to use the phone. He pressed the button that summoned a dispatcher to the other side of his line and identified himself as a New York City police detective. Chemah initially tried a friendly approach to persuade the dispatcher to give him the address where the limo driver was directed to take his wife.

When that didn't work, he threatened to go to the dispatch office and arrest the person for obstructing an investigation. The information he needed was completely forthcoming after that. Chemah had snatched a pen and yellow sticky pad from the desk preparing to get an address to where he would find his wife. When the dispatcher informed him that she was dropped off in front of the W Hotel, Chemah put the pen down and walked out of Kat's office without saying another word.

Kat was scared. She took up the receiver that Chemah put down and dialed her boss' cell number. She received the same response Chemah had gotten: voice mail.

Chapter 27
FILM AT ELEVEN

The receptionist at the W Hotel was reluctant to give Chemah an extra key to the room that his wife had rented, as he had not seen him when his wife had checked into the room. It didn't take Chemah long to convince the man that his wife had rented the room for both of them, and had planned a romantic afternoon interlude. The receptionist understood as he himself had planned many of these occasions with his own wife.

After heading up the elevator, Chemah slipped the key card into the door of the hotel suite smoothly and entered the suite's first room like a silent storm ready to wreak havoc. He was disappointed not to find anyone in the main room as his body was taut with the need to release his anger. Chemah heard grunts and groans coming from the direction of a room to his right and strode purposely toward it. His anger toward Margarita now doubled at the thought that she would have the audacity to be having sex with another man after all the shit she had put him through. His ego had never allowed him to suspect that Margarita would ever cheat on him. He gave her all the sex she ever wanted and he thought he was pretty damn good, too.

Chemah peered through the partially opened door and could only make out the edge of an unmade bed. He stepped carefully and slid through the doorway without bothering to open it any further; not to be detected before he wanted to be. Once inside he was confronted by an almost comical sight. A lone figure lying face down cuffed and shackled to the bed. The stark white figure on the bed turned and fixed scared, dilated pupils on Chemah, and the two recognized each other at precisely the same moment. Chemah walked toward the man prepared to release him from the binding chains. The fear in Dennis' eyes grew to a proportion that made him appear to be a caricature more than a real person.

Bad instincts told him to start pleading right away. "Please, Chemah, don't hurt me. It wasn't my fault," Dennis began.

Chemah's better instincts told him to play along. Chemah sat on the edge of the bed taking a passive aggressive posture. "Why should I believe it wasn't your fault?" Chemah said venomously. He didn't know what was going on here, but he knew that if he played his cards right, this man would tell him everything he needed to know.

Dennis opened his mouth to speak and Chemah put a silent finger to his lips. "The moment I feel you're telling me one untruth, your ass won't be worth a damn," Chemah said. He removed his finger in a dramatically slow manner and said, "Now start from the beginning and don't leave out any details."

Dennis felt his mouth go dry when he heard Chemah's threat. He had never seen Chemah do any physical harm but had heard he was quite capable. To further worsen his plight, the way he was trussed up at this time would put him at the mercy of anyone who had a reason to do his body or reputation damage. Dennis didn't know how much Chemah knew, but it was evident to him that he had to know a good deal to have found him in this hotel room. It would do him no good to hold back any information now. First, he had to get himself out of danger. Then, if he had to deny any wrongdoing later, he would just deny everything.

"When I got the news that it was your son's mother that was murdered, I pulled out all the stops to get the crime solved. I added extra detectives to the case, extra patrol officers, and I wanted all of the evidence to pass through my hands first. After all, I was a professional friend of your wife and you're one of our most highly decorated detectives. It just made good sense."

Chemah nodded his head giving Dennis the okay to continue his story. "Anyway I happen to be in the room when one of the detectives was viewing a surveillance tape and I recognized your wife in it right away."

Chemah interrupted Dennis' story. "That's not possible; the building the crime occurred in didn't have surveillance cameras."

"That's right, they didn't," Dennis confirmed for him, "but the building across the street did have exterior cameras pointed toward the street. That's how I saw Margarita." As mad as Chemah was at Margarita right now, he still didn't like the familiar way Dennis said her name. "I thought it might have been a coincidence," Dennis continued, "but before you got to the station house that day, I asked her if she had ever been to the woman's house before or in the area. She denied knowing anyone that lived in that area; that's how I became suspicious. I decided I'd take possession of the tape before anyone decided to take a second look at it. There were so many tapes I knew no one would miss the one. And if they did, no one would suspect I did it. Honestly, Chemah I was just trying to help Margarita out. I knew there must be a reason why she didn't want anyone to know she was in the area, and knowing her political affiliations, I could only guess that it would be bad publicity for her firm if she were even suspected of wrongdoing."

Chemah nodded again for him to continue. "I called your wife and told her about the tape that I had in my possession. Honestly, I only called her to give her an opportunity to explain it to me before I decided if I had to do anything with it. You know how the media can screw things up once they get a hold of something like this, Chemah." When Chemah didn't acknowledge his logic, Dennis decided it best to continue his story. "When I called her, she suggested we meet here in this hotel. Downstairs in the restaurant," he reiterated, not wanting to suggest that Chemah's wife intentionally invited him to a hotel to have sex. "Once your wife explained that she had visited your son's mother on that day but had nothing to do with her murder, I believed her. You know, your wife and I worked on different political campaigns together before any of this happened, I knew she wasn't capable of anything like that."

Chemah wondered how a man this stupid could have been a detective, but remembered how many other detectives were made by who they knew, not their ability. Dennis wasn't anxious to get to the part of how he began fucking this man's wife and stalled trying to think of how to continue.

"Then what happened?" Chemah said.

"Your wife wanted the copy of the tape that I had. He was afraid that if something were to happen to me, it would get into the wrong hands. We were drinking a lot that night while we were talking it over. I didn't want to give the tape up because I didn't know where the investigation would eventually lead. You know how things can turn, Chemah." He was still trying to get Chemah to identify with him.

"You mean you wanted to see how the tape could help you with your political aspirations," Chemah checked him.

"No, no I was only thinking about her. If any suspicion came to her, we could use it to prove she wasn't there."

"Did you ever check the time that Margarita was across the street from the scene of the crime against the time that forensics said the murder occurred?" Chemah asked.

Dennis closed his eyes as if in pain and shook his head no.

"Then I can only surmise that you didn't care to solve the crime, but only had your own gains in mind," Chemah accused.

Dennis' eyes squeezed closed tighter, steeling himself for the blow that he felt Chemah was working himself up to deliver. When the blow didn't come he opened his eyes and looked at Chemah quizzically. Chemah looked back at the man and couldn't hide the contempt that he felt for him.

Dennis saw the look and thought he had been successful in receiving a modicum of pity. He thought now would be the best time to introduce how he had come to this point. "It's really like I was saying, we were drinking a lot that night. I was making a lot of bad decisions. Margarita's firm already had this room reserved, so we came upstairs to rest and finish our drinks. It wasn't planned or anything; it just happened," he lied. "And you can think what you want," Dennis said indignantly when he saw the now blatant look of disgust on Chemah's face. "This was no tawdry affair. We really felt something for one another."

Chemah almost laughed aloud as Dennis spoke the words. The absurdity of what he spoke aloud, while being trussed up like some wild animal, didn't immediately come to him. When it did dawn on him, he continued with his story in haste. "We've met here a few other times. Nothing like this ever happened before."

"What is it exactly that happened here?" Chemah asked, already surmising what had occurred.

"I think she slipped me some sort of date-rape drug. The last thing I remember before coming to, is that we were having drinks. Then I wake up and I'm all tied up. She told me that if I don't give her the tape of her at the crime scene, she'll show videos of me having sex to everybody. Look at how she tied me up; there's no telling what she did to me while I was unconscious," he said guiltily, feeling the cool air against his anus.

"So you gave her the tape?" Chemah asked.

"I told her where it is; I was going to give it to her today anyway." This time Dennis was telling the truth. He had put the tape in his glove compartment and was going to give it to her as he professed his love for her. This was in the hopes that she would leave her husband to be with him. He decided it was best that he leave that part out.

"Where did you tell her the tape is?"

"I told her it's in my car," Dennis informed him. Chemah digested this information before he decided on his next tack. He knew Margarita well enough to know that she wouldn't bring the tape back to the hotel once she got it. He knew she'd either bring the tape back to the house or dispose of it on the spot.

Chemah knew it didn't matter if he had the tape as proof or not. He didn't need it to prove that she had murdered Nairobi. The fingerprint and blood sample would be enough to convict her in any court of law. Earlier he hadn't known if he had the conviction to take his wife to jail once he confronted her with what he knew, but looking at the pathetic man chained to the bed made his anger well up in his gut. It didn't take much to convince himself that the man deserved a fate worse than just snapping his neck and leaving him there to die. That would be too easy. And a man like this didn't deserve his pity.

Chemah stood up from the bed so abruptly that it startled Dennis. He had closed his eyes tightly again, preparing for the blow he knew he would have delivered, if he had been in the same situation. When the blow didn't come, he opened his eyes and was startled to see that Chemah was dialing a number on his cell phone.

"Are you going to let me out of these chains?" Dennis asked.

"No," Chemah answered coldly as he put the phone to his ear. Dennis allowed his full weight to slump helplessly into the mattress he lay upon and awaited his fate. As he listened to the conversation that developed between Chemah and the person on the other end, he began to wonder if Chemah wouldn't kill him if he begged enough.

"Hello. WNBC News, how can I help you?"

"Hello, can I speak to Judith Lee-Sing, please?" Chemah asked.

"Who should I say is calling?" said the female voice.

"Chemah Rivers." Chemah tried to sound unimpressed.

"Hold on, Mr. Rivers, I'll see if she's taking any calls."

Judith Lee-Sing was the WNBC news producer who had covered the last two cases that Chemah had helped solve. She had called him on other occasions when she needed his expertise to write copy for her news anchors. After approximately ten seconds of waiting, a female voice with a faint British accent came on the line. "Hello, Judith Lee-Sing speaking."

"Hello, Miss Lee-Sing, it's Chemah Rivers."

"Hello, Chemah," she said, losing her professional tone. "To what do I owe this pleasure?"

"I thought I'd give you the heads-up on a breaking news story. A detective giving a news producer a lead on a story, Chemah. What's your angle, detective?"

"No angle, Miss Lee-Sing, just a story," Chemah answered.

"Well then, what's the story?" the producer asked.

"I can't tell you over the phone, Miss Lee-Sing. What I will tell you," Chemah said, "is that it involves a high-ranking police official and some illicit behavior."

"What if I say I'm not interested unless I get more details?" she asked.

"Then I'd say, I'll call Brenda Blackmon and make her the same offer," Chemah countered. "And I'm sure you'll regret your decision in the morning, Miss Lee-Sing."

"No need to make idle threats, Chemah," the soft British voice said. "What do you need for me to do?"

"Come to the W Hotel as fast as you can and bring a camera crew. I'm going to leave a key for you at the front desk. Just come up to the room with the camera and the first part of your story will be waiting for you," Chemah said.

"The first part of the story? How many parts are there?"

Chemah almost lost his patience at the woman's persistent questioning. He had to remind himself that it was her instincts as a journalist that had prompted him to call her to begin with. "Everything will be revealed in due time, Miss Lee-Sing. Just please do as I ask."

Judith Lee-Sing hadn't gotten to where she was in the news business by letting opportunities pass. She knew that when it came to crime stories Chemah was the real deal. He knew things other people didn't, so she listened to what he said, and planned to do what she was told. "I'll be there," she finally relented.

Chemah folded his phone and put it in his hip pocket. He looked down at the bed and saw Dennis weeping like a little girl. He felt no remorse for the phone call he had just made. He thought for the first time that this is what it's like to have ice in your veins.

"See you later, Dee," he said as he walked past the bed and toward the door.

"Don't just leave me like this!" Dennis screamed. "You could at least cover my ass."

Chemah thought for a moment and said over his shoulder, "Pride is a crutch for the insecure." He'd tried to say it like Grandmaster Sam McGee had said it, but it didn't come out quite right. Halfway out the door he changed his mind and walked back toward the still weeping man. Standing over Dennis, Chemah raised his hand above his head, poised for an iron palm strike. Chemah let his hand fall so rapidly that it made a sharp whistling sound right before it struck Dennis in his left buttock. The loud cracking noise his hand made against Dennis' buttock was quickly followed with what could be called a bitch's scream. Chemah looked at Dennis' buttock in satisfaction as he saw a complete and purple imprint of his hand take shape.

Chemah laughed out loud and walked out of the room. Dennis' scream continued to follow him as he went down the elevator. *He really does sound like a bitch,* Chemah thought.

Chapter 28
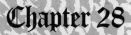

NOW YOU SEE IT, NOW YOU DON'T

Margarita noticed Chemah's BMW parked in front of their home and was about to jet out, when she chanced a look toward the house and saw Chemah staring into her face from the living room window. Margarita smiled and waved to him. Chemah returned a weak smile, and waved back.

It was an unusual time for Margarita to be home. She began to spin a yarn in her head about forgetting some paperwork in the house and having to pick it up and leave quickly for another meeting. She had left Dennis in the hotel room by himself. It wouldn't do to have the hotel cleaning staff walk into the room when no one answered the door and find him naked and shackled to the bed.

Margarita carefully parked her Jag behind Chemah's car. As she walked up to the house she finished all of the details of the lie in her head that she would tell Chemah. She began fingering the keys to the house as she approached the door. She took her time thinking that Chemah had left the window to open the door for her. She waited a few seconds and when Chemah didn't come, she slid the key into the cylinder and opened the door. Chemah wasn't waiting for her in the living room as she had expected when he didn't open the door for her. Margarita stroked the handbag she was clutching; gaining assurance from the tape she had in the bag. She was sure it was the only thing that could stand between her and jail.

Margarita was now curious about where Chemah was and why he hadn't greeted her at the door. "Honey, I'm home," she called out in mock imitation of a television program she watched as a child. She couldn't recall if it was *Leave It to Beaver* or *Father Knows Best*.

When Chemah didn't answer immediately, she went into the kitchen to look for him. When she saw he wasn't there, she grabbed a small steak knife from the dish rack. There was an eerie silence in the house. Still dealing with the paranoia of having the tape in her bag, she thought her husband must have been attacked by an intruder in the house. She assumed the attitude of a predator, concealing the knife she carried in her sleeve. Margarita would kill anyone who had harmed her husband. She slowly climbed the stairs of her home moving stealthily until she reached the top of the stairs. She heard a noise coming from her bedroom, and decided to give the intruder another opportunity to leave.

"Chemah, are you home?" she shouted.

"I'm in here," Chemah called to her from their bedroom.

Shit, Margarita thought. Chemah had given her a scare. Her mindset returned to one of self-preservation. *I hope he's not thinking we're having an afternoon fuckfest.* Margarita touched her vagina through her skirt and winced at its soreness. She had used Dennis' penis; indiscriminately riding it after taking off the shackles so that she could have his penis point toward the ceiling. She had gotten off on raping him with her plastic penis and then using his steel-hard penis any way that she wanted to with her vagina. *Maybe it was too much fun,* she thought, feeling the hurt between her legs again as she walked the last few steps down the hallway that led to her bedroom.

Chemah had taken the liberty of packing a small bag for Margarita. It consisted of new underwear that she kept in her dresser, pajamas, a new toothbrush, jeans, sneakers, a sweat shirt, and deodorant. Margarita walked in as he was closing the bag and asked the most obvious question. "Going somewhere?"

"No," Chemah answered without immediately offering anything else.

"What's the bag for?" She now felt that as if she really didn't want the answer to the question she had just asked.

"The bag's for you."

"Where am I going?" she said, already feeling a little queasy.

"You're going to jail." He finally turned to face her.

Margarita opened her mouth to protest, but nothing came out. She was finally at a loss for words. There was a long silence that lingered like a bad odor. In time, Chemah saw a single tear roll down Margarita's face. The tear didn't extol any sympathy from Chemah, but prompted him to answer the unasked questions.

"You left a fingerprint at Nairobi's place. We couldn't figure out who it belonged to. We checked all the data banks and nothing came up, but like any other criminal you finally made a mistake. The fingerprints that were sent to Albany for your new position as a Commissioner identified you as the person we were looking for." Chemah had worked himself up so much in his indictment of Margarita that he did not notice that the second tear that would have fallen from her eye instantly crystallized and then absorbed back into her body when he compared her to a criminal. "Did you really think you'd get away with this?" Chemah sounded sad.

Margarita's eyes were clear of any moisture when she opened her mouth to answer. She didn't have to think hard to find the words she thought would cut Chemah. She knew the first cut should be the deepest. "I didn't kill her," Margarita said under her breath. All of a sudden a dam seemed to break in her head and she screamed. "That bitch is dead because of you, Chemah! If you hadn't brought her white-bread ass into our lives she'd still be alive right now."

Chemah didn't react to her words. He was used to the histrionics of murderers. Transference of blame was a way for them to rationalize their actions. Chemah allowed her to keep talking; he knew that she would fill in the pieces of the puzzle that the police could not uncover.

Margarita paced the floor in front of her dresser holding handfuls of her own hair in her two fists. "She pushed me first; I swear to God she pushed me first." She sounded as if she were trying to convince herself. "I just went there to leave a new teddy bear for Tatsuya. I called the number that you had for her on the refrigerator and her office told me she was off for the day. I was already on the road so I decided to leave it for him, so that he'd have it when he came home from school. I thought she'd have me leave it downstairs with the doorman, but the bitch actually had the nerve to invite me upstairs. Like we were best buddies or something. She invited me into the apartment and then wanted to show me where I could leave the bear on Tatsuya's bed.

"When I picked up his old teddy bear and told her that I would get rid of it, she flipped, saying how I couldn't replace her with a new teddy bear. As if I actually believed I could. Then she demanded that I put that ratty old teddy bear back on his bed. When I didn't do it fast enough she tried to snatch it from me. That's where the blood came from. We played tug of war with it for a second and then she swung at me. If I hadn't blocked my face she would have scarred me. It was enough that she scratched my hand. I should've knocked that bitch out on the spot, but I held my head and decided I would be a lady.

"That's when she asked me to leave," she continued. "I started to leave that smelly apartment. The smell of wet dog almost overwhelmed me anyway. But I decided to tell her the truth before I left. I told her that you and I were planning to take her to court for custody of Tatsuya. I was telling her how happy we were as a family. You, me, and Tatsuya. I told her she'd still be able to visit him. That's when she started pushing me. Why'd she have to push me? Why'd that bitch have to push me?" Margarita stopped in front of the mirror and yelled at herself.

Margarita turned to Chemah, pleading. "I didn't push her back that hard. She slipped. It wasn't my fault."

"Was she still alive when you left the house, Margarita?"

She was still lucid enough to know where Chemah was leading her with his question. "She was still breathing when I left her," Margarita said unrepentantly.

"She was still breathing as she lay on the floor bleeding into her own brain, and you didn't call for an ambulance?" Chemah said, accusing her with his question.

"I was bleeding, too." Margarita held up her right index finger to show a scratch not visible to the naked eye. She smirked, then pouted like a child in a chilling display of sociopathic indifference. Margarita's acting incensed Chemah. He only now recognized how good an actress Margarita was. He had been a fool from the beginning of their relationship. Led around like a puppy on a leash. His love for Nairobi collided into his fresh hatred for Margarita and scrambled his senses enough to make him blind with rage.

Chemah lunged at Margarita, intent on crushing the smile from her face. And he would have, if he hadn't first felt the knife she had concealed in her sleeve slip between his ribs and into his right lung. As he pulled away from the knife, he felt the air leave his body through the small opening the knife had made. Chemah was going into shock as he fell to the floor clutching his side.

Margarita stood over him still holding the knife in front of her. "I love you, Chemah, but I'm not going to jail for protecting myself against some white bitch that was trying to steal my family."

Chemah's mind was racing. He had allowed his emotions to lead him and had literally killed himself by impaling himself on Margarita's knife. She felt no pity for Chemah; his ego wouldn't allow him to believe the truth. She could almost read his thoughts, and knew he was blaming himself for the stab that she had incurred. Yes, it was he who had jumped on the knife, but it was she who had hidden her intentions until the final moment. That was the key to all martial arts, he had once explained to her. "Free yourself from emotion and you can hide your intention," he had told her. She had been an expert in this art before he had explained how it interpreted into martial arts. She had found it was quite easy to do.

She would have a hard time explaining to the police how she had killed her husband in self-defense. She would have to knock herself around a bit; maybe even break her own arm. Her ace in the hole was Dennis. She would have him lead the investigation in her favor. All she had to do was wait for Chemah to die before she called the police. It was going to be hard, but she quickly made up her mind and knew she would follow it through.

Chemah looked up into Margarita's face and saw his death in her eyes. He grimaced at the pain in his side and decided to rest a second before attempting to get up one final time.

Margarita sat on the bed to wait and decided to turn on the television set. Margarita was watching Judge Judy's television program for about twenty seconds when the news cut to a teaser for the five o'clock news. It showed Dennis as she had left him shackled and cuffed in the hotel room. An authoritative female voice accompanied the clip. "Police captain involved in sordid sex scandal, today on the five o'clock news." His private parts were digitally hidden in the clip, but his scared face was quite visible on the screen.

Margarita looked from the television to where Chemah was attempting to stand up and became stricken with fear. In her fright she rushed at Chemah with the knife in her hand and sealed her fate as she attempted to plunge it into him at her own will. As it came within inches of Chemah's body, the knife turned and left the grasp of her hand as if it had a mind of its own. The coldness of the knife entering her neck did not startle Margarita.

She had known somewhere in the back of her mind what would happen if she attempted to stab Chemah without his volition. It had been a form of suicide, she thought, as she lay bleeding. Images of the times she had witnessed Chemah repel attacks swam through her consciousness as everything slowly turned to black.

Chapter 29
PROBABLE CAUSE

Margarita hired a good lawyer who convinced twelve of her peers that she was not directly responsible for Nairobi's death. She was convicted of manslaughter, and attempted murder. Her lawyer cut a deal and she was sentenced to five years on each account; not to run concurrent with each other for a total of ten years. She was waiting at Rose M. Singer Women's House of Detention on Rikers Island to be transferred to a state institution when the contractions started.

Margarita was looking between her own legs at a small protruding head. It had taken every ounce of her strength to push this much of a baby out of her body. When the doctor announced that she could rest for a second before her last push to get the shoulders, along with the rest of the baby out, she was thankful for the reprieve.

"Alright now, one final push, Margarita," the doctor announced before Margarita was ready. She inhaled deeply and bore down on her womb. She felt a rip and thought, *I've just been torn from my ass to my elbow!* There was a loud sucking noise intermingled with Margarita's scream. "Aieeeeeeeeeeeah," Margarita shrieked until she heard the wail of the newborn that came from her torn loins. The baby was taken from the doctor by a nurse and carried to a table to be cleaned. Margarita lay back and listened to the doctor talk her through the afterbirth that came out.

Minutes later the doctor completed the final suture that would hold her lower extremities together and Margarita saw the nurse standing behind the doctor, holding a small bundle. "Would you like to hold your baby, Mrs. Rivers?" the nurse asked.

Margarita knew this moment would come, but hadn't known how she would react until now. Margarita extended her arms out to the nurse and received the child that God had found fit to bless her with. She held the small bundle tightly and looked down into its angelic face.

The nurse, who was watching Margarita the whole time, saw the confused and questioning look in Margarita's eyes and misread her thoughts. "It's a girl," the nurse spoke out of turn.

Margarita looked up at the nurse, cursing her with her eyes. She looked back down at her baby and marveled at the crystal blue eyes that stared up at her. The child's skin was translucent and milky. On a whim she pulled the skull cap from the baby's head and smiled at the golden wisps of blonde hair atop her head. Margarita didn't laugh out loud at God's little joke, but was amused nonetheless. She placed the skull cap back on top of the baby's head and began to rock her gently. She already felt a fierce instinct to protect the child. Margarita was reluctant to let the baby go when the nurse returned for her.

"You need your rest," the nurse cautioned. The nurse was a large Hispanic woman with wide hips and a big mouth. Margarita had fussed with her earlier and thought better than to antagonize her again. "Here we go, baby," the nurse spoke to the cooing child as she pulled her to her bosom. "Let's let your mommy rest and we'll come back later when you're ready to eat," she said, walking out of the room.

"Mommy," Margarita said aloud, trying her new and official title on for size. She knew it was a short-term title. Before long they would be taking her upstate to do a ten-year bid, and there would be no place in the penitentiary for a baby. She had tried for so long to get pregnant, that when she found out nine months ago while waiting for trial that she was pregnant, there was no question as to whether she would keep it or abort.

She and her counselor at the jail had gone over all of the possibilities for who would get the child when she had to be sent away. She had considered it a long shot that the child might belong to Dennis, but still never considered him a prospect as a guardian for her child.

Dennis had lost his job when the whole affair was aired. His wife had left him, and the department had filed formal charges against him for withholding evidence. The last thing she had heard was that he could be receiving jail time. Her father was getting on in years. She was sure he would take the child if she asked, but she thought of the life the child would lead in another country, and the prospect of never seeing the child again until she was released. As many times as she went over it in her head, she always came up with the same answer: Chemah.

She hadn't seen him since he testified early in the trial. Her stomach hadn't been showing back then, so he never knew that she was pregnant. The trial had taken six months and through it all he had refused to take her phone calls.

Afraid that the child would have to be sent to a foster home or worse, adopted if she couldn't find someone to take her, she begged Kat to go see him on her behalf. Kat was not to give him any details as to the reason why she needed so desperately to see him—only that it was a matter of life and death.

There was no question in Margarita's mind whether Chemah would take custody of a child that they had made together. He had lost the opportunity to help raise Tatsuya in his formative years and she knew he would not allow that to happen with a child of his again. Unfortunately that was not the case. She didn't know any man that would raise a child alone that was not his. She didn't have a leg to stand on with Chemah, but for her child's sake she would beg him if she had to. God had thrown shit into the game with the blonde hair and blue eyes. She wondered if she was legally bound to tell Dennis that they had a child together.

Chapter 30
MY BABY DOES THE HANKY-PANKY

At the precise moment Margarita fell asleep, Kat was ringing the doorbell to the brownstone still owned by her now convict friend. Chemah would not listen to Kat. He turned a deaf ear to her desperate pleas on behalf of her homegirl. She had finally caught up with him at home and now after a stormy argument had informed him through tear-stained eyes that Margarita was "with child."

"How does she know it's my baby?" Chemah asked, sick with the thought of a child of his being born in jail.

"Who else's would it be?" Kat spat before she had reasoned her response.

Chemah glowered at her and bit his lip to stop himself from cursing her. Tatsuya was in the living room and it would not do for him to hear the foul language that he was thinking right now.

Undaunted, Kat continued to light into him. "Well, you'll never know if you don't go see her and find out for yourself." Chemah knew she was right but it didn't make him feel any better.

Two days later he made arrangements to see Margarita at the Woman's Detention Center. When he arrived he was told that she'd had a baby two days earlier and was still on the hospital ward. Chemah's status as a detective allowed him privileges not normally afforded other visitors. A corrections officer was assigned to him as an escort and he was allowed to move about freely as long as the officer traveled with him.

Margarita was sitting up in her bed when he entered the dorm room that housed five other women that had recently given birth. He accepted that there would be no privacy, save that which could be gained by whispering your entire conversation. Margarita saw the starch he had pressed into his back as he walked through the dormitory door and did not delude herself into thinking this would be an amicable visit. Margarita motioned for Chemah to sit on the chair that had been placed on the side of her bed. Chemah shook his head no and considered offering it to the escorting corrections officer who had discreetly stood by the door to allow for more privacy.

Margarita thought best to just come out with it. "I have a favor to ask of you."

"I didn't come here to grant any favors," Chemah said, fighting to keep control of his emotions. This was the woman that he had slept with for many years. A woman he shared secrets with. A woman who tried to kill him and the woman who had murdered the true love of his life. He wouldn't be able to bear being in the same room with her too much longer. "All I want to know is, is it mine?"

"It's a little girl," Margarita said, holding off Chemah's query.

Chemah was shaken by the softness in her voice. He felt a momentary feeling of hope. "Is it my little girl?" he said, finally daring to have a good thought about Margarita.

She swung her legs over the side of the bed and stood up in front of Chemah; she was ready to fall at his feet and beg a chance at a decent life for her child when she told him the worst truth. "The baby isn't yours, Chemah."

When the words first came out of her mouth, they didn't immediately register. After a moment, the words she spoke became clear to him and he momentarily thought he should find the seat that he had initially refused. Instead he turned on his heel and headed for the exit door, trying to get away from Margarita. She attempted to grab Chemah's arm, but was thwarted by the officer who had anticipated there might be an altercation when Margarita came off the bed. "Mrs. Rivers, please go back to your bed," he said, leading Margarita by the arm to the bed.

The nurse was wheeling Margarita's baby into the room and almost bumped into Chemah as he was walking out. Chemah tried not to look at the child as he passed her, but was drawn to look at the baby the way people on the highway can't help but take their turn looking at the twisted masses of metal at a car collision. It wasn't an immediate recognition as much as it was an odd sort of déjà vu. Chemah could have sworn he had seen that little face before and as he turned around in an attempt to get a second look, it occurred to him where he had seen it.

When Nairobi showed him pictures of Tatsuya as a baby, he had looked just like the baby that had just passed him. Not to mention the similarities to his own baby pictures. The story of how his father had questioned his mother as to why his son was born with blue eyes and blonde hair was a favorite around Christmas every year. He had never known his grandmother, but his mother had explained how she was the only family member besides him who had the very light-brown hair and green eyes. His own grandmother had to explain to his father that his child's blue eyes would turn hazel green in time and that his hair would darken, too. They didn't have paternity tests back in those days, and it was only the threat of an ass whuppin' from his grandmother that had stopped his father from continuing to question his second child's ethnicity. As the memory crossed his mind, he turned and walked back into the room.

Margarita was wrestling with the officer who was trying everything in his power not to hurt her, while still not allowing her to get past him. The nurse was waiting with the baby right inside the door as if she had witnessed this scenario many times in the past.

Margarita saw Chemah over the officer's shoulder and stopped struggling. The officer took the opportunity to look over his own shoulder and seemed relieved to see that Chemah had walked back into the room. Everyone seemed to be waiting for him to say something, so he did. "I want a paternity test performed," he said to Margarita.

Margarita wiped the tears from her eyes and nodded her consent. Everyone waited for Chemah to say something else, so he did. "Can I get a clean hospital gown?" he inquired. "I'd like to hold my daughter," he announced proudly.

Epilogue
MEMORIES FADE, BUT THE SKY STILL LINGERS

hemah's daughter, Hèro, was crying for her father to pick her up. She had just come from her first visit with her mother and was still temperamental from the long period of time she had spent in her car seat. Chemah didn't like spoiling the baby, but he could never bear to hear her cry. Tatsuya was always helpful with her and came running with her pacifier before Chemah had a chance to lift her. Hèro took the pacifier, but still stretched her arms out to be lifted.

Chemah wished he had asked Tatsuya's babysitter to stay a little longer. He needed a nap after the long day he had endured with Margarita at the penitentiary. He was loath to subject his baby girl to the conditions at a state prison, but he had no choice. The lawyers Margarita hired were relentless in court. She had gotten visiting rights and guaranteed dual custody contingent upon her release from prison. Looking at Margarita across a table while she played with her daughter had been painful to him.

He felt bad for his son who was at home waiting for him. The little boy had been deprived of a mother by this woman and regardless what the courts convicted her of, he would always hold her responsible for Nairobi's death. Chemah knew that Tatsuya understood everything that occurred within the last year. He was a very smart and inquisitive little boy. When Tatsuya was brought to the hospital to visit him, he'd had to convince him all over again that he would never leave him alone.

When Chemah brought Hèro home he thought he'd have to deal with some sibling rivalry. He wasn't surprised by Tatsuya's good-natured attitude toward his sister, but didn't actually understand it until Tatsuya inadvertently explained it to him on a night that Hèro woke them both out of a fitful sleep. "If we love her enough, Dad, when she finds herself alone, she'll remember us and it'll make her feel better." Chemah couldn't argue with that kind of logic.

He followed Tatsuya's advice and never missed an opportunity to spoil either one of his children. They only had each other now. He would never make the mistake of believing they had forever to be together. He would make every moment they had together count. With that thought, he shrugged off the tired feeling he felt and picked his daughter up.

"Go get your jacket, Tat. We're going out for ice cream."

Chemah felt better now. He knew he was doing all he could.

ABOUT THE AUTHOR

David Rivera, Jr. has been writing short stories for many years and has been inspired by the writings of the contemporary black male writers who have emerged during the past few years. His first book, *Harlem's Dragon,* has been received with great enthusiasm by other writers as well as literary critics. David lives in Harlem, U.S.A. with his family and aspires to reignite the literary flame that Harlem has been renowned for with his debut novel, *Harlem's Dragon,* and its upcoming sequel, *The Street Sweeper.* He received a bachelor's degree in sociology and a master's degree in public administration. David Rivera, Jr. can be contacted at setodavid@aol.com. Visit his web site at www.davidriverajr.com.

EXCERPT FROM

The Street Sweeper

BY DAVID RIVERA, JR.

OCTOBER 2006 FROM STREBOR BOOKS

LADY SINGS THE BLUES

Margarita was in her cell contemplating the last four years of her life. She looked at herself in the shiny piece of metal acting as a mirror that hung on her wall. Her hair had finally grown back to its normal shoulder length. Her dark brown skin was radiant today, she thought. It was a testament of how she felt inside. Her body felt strong now after lifting weights daily for three years, as opposed to when she first arrived and had the slim figure of a model.

Her jail family had been coming by all day in a steady stream of visitors: mostly the Spanish women who had taken her in and protected her when they found out she was Panamanian, and the younger women of color she had protected thereafter. She had been denying her heritage most of her life, and here in the penitentiary, speaking Spanish had saved her. She hadn't known what to expect, but after three years in the penal system she'd become a pro at maneuvering around and through the bullshit. She didn't like to think about it now that she knew she'd be getting out soon, but if she'd had to spend her life in here she knew she could run the whole prison.

As it now stood, she had wrested a considerable amount of power from one of the toughest bitches in the whole prison. She considered the life of the woman named Lolly. The woman who had befriended her on her first day in the system and had turned her out on that very same night. The woman who now lay in the hospital dying from wounds that Margarita had inflicted.

✠✠✠

On her first day in the pen, Margarita was nervous and apprehensive about what to expect. She'd been sitting in a corner of the day room watching television with other inmates when a giant bull dyke named Charli had approached her and unceremoniously had informed her that she'd be the one eating her cunt out that night and every other night after that. Margarita was well aware that this type of behavior occurred in female prisons as she had witnessed it during the year she'd spent on Rikers Island while going through trial. During that time, when she'd been invited to participate in a lesbian act, she'd just told the person that she was not interested and they'd go away.

When Margarita told Charli that she wasn't interested, Charli eased up next to her and began to whisper nasty shit in her ear that she was going to do to her. Although Margarita was afraid of the woman, she knew she had to take a stand before it went any further. Margarita got up from her seat, determined to face Charli down; Charli anticipated the move and got up right along with her. Charli was a full foot taller than Margarita and looked down at her menacingly. Before Margarita was able to say anything, Lolly had strolled up alongside her and addressed Charli.

Lolly was approximately Margarita's height but had a more muscular build as if she worked out with weights regularly. She wore her hair in two plaits and if it weren't for the scar over her left eye, she'd have had the face of a model.

"Are we having a problem here?",Lolly said, putting an arm around Margarita's shoulder as if they had been buddies for years.

Charli looked shaken, and answered Lolly before actually having gained her composure. "No, Lolly, we're not having any problem. Are we, sweetheart?" She directed her question at Margarita.

"No, no problem at all," Margarita answered, not wanting any further problems.

Lolly continued to stare up at Charli until she looked so uncomfortable that she looked away and changed her posture. Shifting her weight from her left side to her right and then back again. "If you don't have anything else to say, then move the fuck along, Lurch." Lolly said to the bigger woman.

Charli had a hurt look in her eye and bit her lip the way women do when they're trying to stop themselves from crying. The big woman that had up until that moment been portraying herself as the most masculine thug, had now been reduced to the basest example of a weak, emotional and sniveling woman with just a few words and a look from Lolly.

"Sorry about that," Lolly said, taking her arm from around Margarita's shoulder as she took notice of her discomfort. "Don't worry about her. She won't bother you again if she knows you and I are friends."

Lolly introduced herself to Margarita and after lunch introduced her to the rest of the set she belonged to. Or the way Margarita observed it, the set that belonged to Lolly. Margarita followed Lolly around the rest of the day. When it was time for Lolly to report to her work detail, she told Margarita to join her. Margarita was leery of going as she didn't want to get into any beef with the corrections officers about being in an unauthorized area.

It took Lolly a minute to convince her that it would be no problem. True to her word, the C.O.'s said nothing to either one of the women as Lolly greeted the C.O. in the laundry room with a nod of her head.

Margarita's political background had accustomed her to being in the presence of persons that wielded power and she easily recognized the deference of the people who dealt with Lolly.

After evening chow, Margarita was tired and decided she would lock in. Lolly tried to get her to hang out in the day room, but Margarita begged off and went back to her cell to sleep.

The singular *click* of a lone cell door opening was tantamount to a bell ringing in the middle of a library. It was unnatural in this place where all doors opened and closed simultaneously. Margarita's eyes opened immediately, but she did not make any noise or move. She feared she would give away some advantage. She couldn't tell what time it was because there was no window that she could peer out of to gauge the moonlight. Margarita heard feet shuffling in her cell before she heard the voice.

"Margarita. Pssst, Margarita, are you awake?"

Relief passed over Margarita as she recognized Lolly's voice. She smiled to herself at her own paranoia and flipped over in her bunk, glad to greet her new friend. Margarita's smile turned to shit as she turned around and looked into the faces of four women. Lolly's face was one of them. The big dyke Charli was another and she did not recognize the final two. Lolly was holding an ice pick under Margarita's neck and her lips were curled into a twisted, sadistic smile. The other three women jeered at Margarita over Lolly's shoulder, looking like hyenas waiting their turn at the slaughter of a lamb.

"Make one sound, bitch, and I shove this through your mouth and into your brain. You understand me."

Margarita silently nodded her head, and the gesture made Lolly's smile broaden.

"Sit up," she ordered Margarita. She did her bidding and sat up slowly, afraid to be poked by the cold piece of steel against her skin. "Take her clothes off of her," Lolly ordered the women behind her, stepping slightly to the side but always keeping the ice pick under Margarita's chin.

Margarita closed her eyes as the women pounced on her. They took her pajama pants off first, then her top, and finally her panties.

"Now let's see those tits," Margarita heard Lolly's voice say as she felt a cold hand reach behind her back and unsnap the fastener of her bra.

"Mmmm, damn, those are pretty," one of the unidentified women said as the bra fell.

After a moment, Margarita felt a weight other than her own on the bed. Then came a sickeningly sweet whisper from Lolly. "Open your eyes, Margarita. I have something for you, baby." Margarita heard the other women snicker and then she opened her eyes. Margarita stared into Lolly's shaved vagina. It was a fat drooling cunt. The lips were swollen and hanging open. In the dimly lit cell, Margarita could make out the tattoo right above Lolly's pierced clitoris. It read "POISON."

Margarita's eyes bugged at the sight and she shook her head from side to side in disbelief of her predicament.

Lolly was delighted at her response and whispered to her again. "You can't believe your good luck, can you, baby? First night on the tier and already you get a sample of the prettiest pussy in the pen. Oh, just one warning, baby," Lolly said menacingly. "If I feel anything more than the playful nibble of your teeth on my pussy, you get this in your ear."

Margarita felt the cold steel play on her earlobe and knew that Lolly was not bluffing. Margarita swallowed the revulsion she felt, as Lolly leaned her hips into her half-open mouth. She felt Lolly's wet fleshy labia brush her lips and before she could move away, Lolly grabbed the back of her head with one hand and pulled it forward into her splayed cunt. Margarita closed her mouth and held her breath while Lolly ground into her face. When Margarita felt her nose slide into Lolly's wildly contracting hole, she was forced to open her mouth to breathe. Lolly continued her wild humping of Margarita's face for a full five minutes. The juices from her cunt were all over Margarita's face dripping from her chin. Lolly's breath was coming in short gasps in time with her hip thrusts. "Uh uh uh uh uh uh uh…stick your tongue out, baby, stick it out."

Remembering the feel of cold steel, Margarita did as she was told. "Uh-huh, uh-huh, here it is, baby, here's Lolly's juice. Aaaaaaaaahhh Shiiiiiiiiiiiiiiiiit!!!" Lolly convulsed into Margarita's face. It seemed to take an eternity for Lolly to stop shaking. Margarita felt herself go limp as Lolly released her head from a vise-like grip. Margarita was glad that the ordeal was over.

"She's all yours, ladies," Margarita heard Lolly announce. At this declaration the two still unidentified women lunged at Margarita. Each woman was holding down one of Margarita's arms and shoulders. Charli was between Margarita's legs before Margarita could get them closed. Margarita looked down between her own legs, willing them to close as Charli used her massive arms to pry them further apart. When Charli seemed to be satisfied they were apart enough, she settled back on her haunches.

Margarita was not mildly shocked when she saw what was fastened onto Charli's waist. It was a thick leather belt with a piece of wood attached to it. Margarita looked hard and was sure it was the end of a broomstick. Charli laughed when Margarita realized her intention and struggled harder against the two women holding her down. When the wood entered her, Margarita didn't scream. She bit her bottom lip until she could taste her own blood. She swore then and there that these women would die by her hand.

✜✜✜

Three of the four women were dead now. Lolly was in the infirmary. They didn't know if she was going to make it. Margarita was loath to leave until she was sure that she had kept her promise to herself. She had done everything she could to get herself an early release. She'd had her lawyer contact powerful people who still owed her favors and other people whose secrets she had kept when she herself was in power. The pressure they'd put on the parole board had been enough to get her out without having to go to the board a second time. She'd done her minimum three years. The warden had questioned everyone personally on the accident that had befallen the tragic three women that died in the fire six months ago. It went on record as just that—an accident.

Lolly, on the other hand, was a different story. Margarita had wanted to see the fear in her eyes as she died. Wanted her to know that she was the one taking her life. Setting Lolly up had been a work of art. Without her three henchmen, Lolly's power had been fragile, and Margarita's jail family had gotten stronger. In the end, it had been easy to catch her alone and plunge a pen into her eye. No one had heard Lolly scream and Margarita had taken her time beating her senseless.

The guard escorting Margarita out of the facility came to her cell. "Are you ready to go, Smith?"

Margarita looked around her cell. She had not packed anything. She wanted no memories of this place.

"I'm ready," Margarita said, stepping out of the cell. "And it's *Ms.* Smith," she said, tossing her hair back, almost striking him in the face. "And don't you forget it."